THE DECEPTIVE TWIN

L.R. JACKSON

Editing By: Julia at Diamond in the Rough Editing

Proofreading By: Sandra at One Love Editing: Cover Image: Adobestock

Cover Design: Anna Crosswell at Cover Couture

Formatting By: Jeff at Indie Formatting

ACKNOWLEDGMENTS

Hey, there! I'd like to thank you for picking up The Deceptive Twin. This story took me on quite the journey, but it was so much fun.

This book would not be what it is without the help and support of everyone involved. First, I'd like to thank my beta readers, Jo Conklin and Rosalee Jesudas. Thank you for your honest feedback and raw critique. I wouldn't have been able to finish this book without it.

I'd like to thank my editor, Julia. Thank you for your inspiring words and your keen eye. You are appreciated more than you know.

Lastly, to you, the reader. I want to take the time to thank you for your support. You have no idea how much it means to have you read my work. You make what I do worth it.

Happy Reading!: L.R. Jackson
xoxo

Want first dibs on release dates and sneak peeks? Sign up for my newsletter below. www.authorlrjackson.com/newsletter

THE DECEPTIVE TWIN

MORGAN

All she was supposed to do was step into her twin's perfect life for a little while and take an opportunity to be the *fun* one for once. To know what it felt like to really *live*. The last thing she ever meant to do was fall for her sister's husband. How can something that is so *wrong* feel so *right*?

JASEN

His wife had become almost like a roommate over the past few years. The distance between them had been insurmountable. Until recently. Something about her is ... different. She's warmer, softer somehow. Jasen is shocked to find himself falling in love with his gorgeous wife all over again. But... is she *really* his wife?

When tragedy strikes, Morgan is forced to choose between continuing the lie and owning up to her deception. Doing the right thing could mean losing the only man she's ever loved, but can a relationship built on betrayal ever truly last? More importantly, will Jasen even want her when he learns the truth—or will the price of forgiveness simply be more than he's willing to pay?

CHAPTER 1

MORGAN: PRESENT DAY

Tears fall heavily as I stare down at the photo in front of me. The body is spread out on the floor. Her right leg curves while her left leg is straight. Her arms lie at her side. Her head is turned to the right, and her eyes are closed, as if she's sleeping. The name **Morgan Vaughn** is written across the bottom of the photo in black.

"I know this must be hard for you."

I don't respond to the detective. Because it's a stupid statement for him to make. Of course this is hard for me. She was my sister.

Jasen squeezes my hand slightly, offering me comfort while I sniffle and wipe away my tears with a tissue. "Take your time, Monroe." I turn to face him, and my tearful eyes meet his sympathetic ones. This is the toughest thing I've ever had to do. Life as I knew it is over. But despite it all, I have *him*. Jasen is an amazing man. He's hardworking, charming, and very handsome with his deep dimples and dark brown eyes. He's at the height

1

of his career as the owner of one of the top private investigating firms in California. He's protective, loving, and reliable.

As pathetic as it sounds, I've never had a man treat me as well as he does. He's everything I could ever want in a husband, but he isn't really *my* husband. He's my sister's husband. He and the detective think it's *me* in that photo. But it isn't. They have no clue that Monroe and I switched places so she could run off with her lover, and that he's been living with his wife's twin sister all this time. At first, I didn't understand why Monroe felt the need to sleep around on Jasen—he worshipped the ground she walked on. She had the perfect life, but she took it for granted. I later found out that she wanted to be free and unattached instead of being confined as a housewife. She wanted to explore her options and see what sex was like outside of the man she had been with since the eleventh grade. Monroe felt the constant urge to feel liberated. But her need to feel liberated came with a cost... her life.

The detective slides the picture back towards him. "How about we do this another time, Mrs. Baker?"

I open my mouth to answer him, but my cell phone rings, interrupting us. I pull my phone out of my purse. It's the call I've been waiting for. "I need to take this," I announce.

Jasen nods. "You go ahead. I'll finish up here."

I grab my bag, step outside, and close the door behind me. I watch Jasen and the detective through the glass window as I answer the call. "Hello."

"Hi, Monroe?"

"Yes."

"This is Dr. Danni. I'm calling to inform you that we received your lab results back this morning and it's confirmed. You're pregnant. Congratulations!"

SIX WEEKS EARLIER

I glance down at my watch for the third time. He's now fifteen minutes late. *Maybe he's not coming.* I lift my head and scan the group of people in the waiting area. I exhale with frustration when I don't see him. Where is he? The door opens again, and in walks a tall man, wearing a black peacoat, black gloves, and a red scarf. It must be him, because he looks similar to the picture on Randy's profile. Randy is the guy I've been interacting with on Match.com for the past two weeks. After nightly phone calls and all-day text messages, we decided it was time for us to meet in person. He chose this place. An upscale, authentic Italian restaurant. I was quite impressed when I arrived. So far, he's checked off all my boxes. Great personality. Check. Sense of humor. Check. Respectful. Check. He's not into playing games or hooking up. He's looking for something serious, just like I am. And to top it off, he's successful. He owns his own technology firm. The host looks in my direction, grabs another menu, and leads him towards my table. As they get closer, I'm blown away. *Holy shit!* He's even sexier in person. He smiles at me, and all frustration disappears. I stand to my feet to greet him, but he walks right past me. I turn around just in time to see Mr. Sexy hug the gorgeous brunette waiting for him at the table behind me. I deflate with anger.

"Morgan?"

My head whips around, and I come face-to-face with a man I don't recognize. He senses my confusion, so he extends his hand. "It's me, Randy."

This can't be Randy. Randy's height is six foot two. The man standing in front of me matches my height of five foot five. Randy has black hair. This man has brown hair. Randy has a beard. This man is clean-shaven. Randy has abs. Toned shoulders and biceps. I know because I drooled over the pictures he posted of himself at the gym. This man? He's chubby. With man boobs and a beer belly. In no way, shape, or form am I making fun of his body. Or judging his appearance. But it isn't fair to mislead a person. I thought the man I was meeting looked... well, nothing like the man standing in front of me.

"I... ahh... I'm sorry I'm late," he stammers.

I cross my arms over my chest. "I almost left."

He nods. "Have a seat, and I'll explain."

I should *not* have a seat. I should grab my purse and leave him where he stands. And not only because he had me waiting, but because I've been duped. But I have absolutely nothing else to do tonight. So, I have a seat across from Mr. Liar. He smiles nervously.

"I'm so sorry. I literally showered and got dressed two hours early, just so I could make it here on time. But when I was walking out the door, I noticed Gramps was looking a little pale. Turns out he missed his insulin shot and was feeling a little sick."

"Gramps?"

"Yeah, my grandfather. We live together."

"You said you live alone," I remind him.

"Well, technically, I do. He lives with me, not the other way around."

I nod and allow him to proceed. "Anyway, I had to get him squared away before I could come."

I realize I'm being too hard on him. It's admirable for him to take care of his elderly grandfather. It shows he's responsible. Compassionate. Caring. Qualities I'm attracted to. I nod. "I understand."

The waitress arrives, and once she takes our orders, he continues to speak. "I guess you're probably wondering why I don't look like my profile pictures."

I grab my glass of water. "It did catch me off guard," I answer right before taking a sip.

"I'm sorry about that. A friend created my profile and

thought it would be funny to post pictures of himself instead of me. I hadn't gotten around to changing them because I honestly didn't take the site seriously at first."

"Sounds like my coworker. She's the one who created my profile. I had no interest in it, but the one time I logged on, I connected with you."

"I'm glad. I've enjoyed talking to you the past few weeks, and I was looking forward to our date tonight."

I smile. "So was I."

The waitress brings us dinner rolls, and we both reach for one. "You're even more beautiful in person."

"Thank you."

There's an awkward silence as we butter our rolls. We steal glances as we chew and smile nervously as we drink our waters. This describes every date I've ever been on. Awkward. Shy. Not knowing what to say. I suck at conversation with the opposite sex. I suck at witty humor and in-depth answers about who I am and what I like to do. I'm fine talking over the phone. We've had the most amazing conversations these past two weeks. But now that the moment is here and we're face-to-face, I've got nothing.

"So, tell me more about your work."

I finish chewing. "I'm just a substitute teacher for now. Hopefully, I'll transition to becoming a full-time teacher soon."

"Sounds like you love what you do."

"I do. I love making a difference."

He nods in agreement. "So do I. It's something about helping people that makes me sleep well at night."

He has a good heart. Shame on me to judge him.

"You have no idea how happy my customers are after they leave with a new phone or new data plan," he continues.

"Your company helps with phone technology?" I ask, eager to hear more. I grab my glass to take another sip.

"Yeah, I mean, we're the number one network in America. You can't get any better with Verizon."

I almost choke on my water. "Excuse me?"

"Are you okay?" he asks with concern.

"I'm fine. You mentioned Verizon. What exactly do you do again?"

He straightens in his seat with pride. "I'm the number one salesman at Verizon store 486. You should swing by sometime. I'll hook you up with a discount."

The waitress brings our food, but I'm too angry to eat. "Thanks for the offer. But I'm good."

"Seriously, you're missing out. I can get you the new iPhone for half the price." He smiles with satisfaction, and I want to stab him with my fork. Was anything in his profile the truth? I start to respond, but my cell phone rings. I glance at the caller. It's my sister, Monroe. I ignore the call and turn my attention back to Randy. *If* that's even his real name. "You told me you own a technology firm."

"I was speaking it into existence. That's the goal eventually. Once I work my way up to manager, I'll be as good as gold."

I place a strand of hair behind my ear as he continues to talk. "I'll have it all one day. A big house. A beautiful wife. A nice car. And I can't wait. Especially for the car. I'm so tired of taking the subway."

"Wait a minute. You said you drive a Mercedes, but it was in the shop. Remember, you offered to pick me up, but I agreed to meet you here instead?"

He waves me off. "Oh yeah, I was going to drive my friend's car, but I accidently rear-ended someone when I was on my way to the sperm bank. Needed the extra bucks, you know?"

My eyes go wide. This is the date from hell. And to make matters worse, my coworker Linda hasn't called me yet to see if I need a date bailout. The waitress places the check beside him, and he reaches in his left pants pocket. He removes his hand, then reaches into the right one. He winces as he pulls an empty hand out. "I must have lost my wallet."

My phone rings again. I grab it quickly, hoping it's Linda so I can pay the damn bill and bail out quickly, but it's Monroe again. "Guess I'm paying," I respond as I pull cash from my purse and place it on the table.

My phone rings again, and this time, I know something must be wrong. I haven't heard from Monroe in months. And she never calls me back-to-back like this.

I stand to my feet. "Excuse me. This might be important."

He nods as I turn and walk quickly to the bathroom. I push the door open and walk inside. I pace back and forth a few times, pissed that Randy has basically wasted two weeks of my time. I should have never agreed to this date. I stop in front of the mirror closest to the door and take a deep breath. I take one glance at my reflection right before I dial Monroe. She picks up on the first ring. "Thank God you called me back."

"What do you want," I reply dryly.

"That's the greeting I get from my own twin?"

"Just answer the question," I reply.

"I need a favor, sissy."

"*You* need a favor from *me?*"

"Yup, and it's a big one."

"What makes you think I would do anything for you after the way you spoke to me?"

There's a moment of silence before she speaks. "Listen, I'm sorry, Mo."

"Don't call me that," I respond.

I never liked the nickname she chose for me, and she knows it. But that's Monroe, always looking to get under my skin somehow.

"Okay. Morgan, I'm sorry for the things I said."

"You're only saying you're sorry because you need me for something."

"No, I'm not. I really am sorry... and I miss you."

I can't deny that I miss her too. I thought about calling her a few times, but there's no way I would give her the satisfaction of me reaching out first. And trust me, she would have gloated about it. But it's been a little over two months, and she's my sister. It's time we make up and reconcile. Besides, this is the longest we've been mad at each other, and I've hated every second of it.

"What's the favor?" I ask.

Monroe instantly becomes excited. "Oh my gosh, I have so much to catch you up on."

"Can't wait."

"How about I book a flight to Philly and we can discuss it then? I'll start packing."

"Wait, you're going to fly here all the way from California, when you can just tell me now?"

"Hell yeah. I haven't spoken to you in months. Besides, what I have to ask of you will require lots of wine."

"Okay. I'll see you soon."

She squeals one last time before ending the call. I fix my hair in the mirror before I head back to my table. I've decided I'm never going to see or speak to Randy again. He's a liar. And I hate liars. I plan to tell him to lose my number. I plan to tell him that what he did was wrong and that playing with people's emotions is immature. Shame on him for catfishing me. By the time I reach the table, I'm furious. So furious, I'm about to give him a piece of my mind. Only I don't get the chance. Because Randy is gone, and so is the money I left on the table.

THREE DAYS LATER

"You're kidding right?" I ask.

I watch Monroe shake her head as she pours us both another glass of red wine. It's way too early for us to be drinking, but she was right—this was a conversation we needed to have over wine. She arrived early this morning and took it upon herself to catch an Uber to the house and let herself in. The downside of living in the family home meant that both of us had access to it at any time.

"You're asking me to fly to California, switch identities, and spend the weekend pretending to be you?" I clarify.

"Yup."

"That won't work, Monroe."

"Yes, it will. Jasen will have no idea," she argues.

My thoughts transition to Jasen Baker. I had such a huge crush on him in high school. I was borderline obsessed with him. He and I shared Chemistry class together as well as English. I spent most of my time in class fantasizing about him. Despite his popularity, Jasen wasn't arrogant or shallow. He was smart, and very friendly. He would say hello to me every single day while everyone else ignored me. I wanted so badly to tell him that I liked him, but I was too nervous to say anything. Besides, I was shy and awkward. He wouldn't have been interested in me anyway.

Monroe learned that I had a crush on him when she barged into my room one night and caught me stalking his Facebook page. I denied it at first. But she didn't believe me. So, I gave in and admitted that I liked him. She knew that I was too shy to tell him, so she offered to get his phone number for me. Needless to say, that didn't happen. I was heartbroken, and I didn't speak to her for days. I felt betrayed and humiliated. If it wasn't for our grandmother, I may have never spoken to her again. I can still hear our grandmother's voice in my ear.

Morgan, boys will come and go, but Monroe will always be your sister. She's the other half of you.

I blink my eyes a few times, bringing my focus back to the conversation. "He'll figure out what we've done. I'm nothing like you," I explain.

It's scary how much we look alike. We share the same fair skin, high cheekbones, and cognac-colored eyes. We both have shoulder-length hair. We're the same height and same size. We both have long shapely legs, slim waists, and round hips. Our grandmother said that we inherited our curvy figures from our mother. Our voices sound the same, we laugh the same, and we have the exact same mannerisms. Even our grandmother would mix us up. But as much as we are alike, we're also vastly different. Monroe is adventurous. Rebellious. She has a certain spunk that draws people to her. And she loves attention. She craves it. She dresses in the shortest skirts, tightest shirts, and highest heels. Women like her and men love her. I'm the conservative twin. The Goody Two-shoes, as some may call it. I'm quiet. Reserved. And I don't flaunt my curves. I cover them modestly. Our grandmother always said that when it came to men, we should leave something to the imagination. I guess Monroe ignored that little tip. I shake my head and remind her again. "We're nothing alike."

"Which is why I came here. I need to teach you to be *me* before we do this, starting with changing your hair and wardrobe."

I frown. "There's nothing wrong with my hair, or my clothes."

"Of course, there isn't. But Jasen is used to seeing me look a certain way."

"And what way is that?"

"I always wear makeup, my hair is always done, and my clothes are always well put together."

I assess my sister. It's early in the morning, and she's wearing an expensive-looking dress, designer shoes of some kind, and a face full of makeup. Not a string of hair is misplaced. Meanwhile, I'm lounging around in sweats and a T-shirt, and my hair is in a bun. I cringe at the thought of wearing designer clothing and makeup *all* the time. I'd much rather be comfortable than stylish.

"This is a bad idea, Monroe. Why do you need me to do this anyway?"

"Because I'm seeing someone else."

My eyes go wide. "You're cheating on Jasen?"

"If that's what you want to call it."

I swallow a gulp of wine. "With whom?"

"With Cooper," she answers.

"Who is Cooper?"

"Cooper is the best lover I've ever had."

I watch my sister while she continues to talk about her lover. She rambles on and on about how much fun they have together and how it's becoming harder and harder to sneak around. Meanwhile, I'm filled with confusion. Jasen has been good to her. They have the perfect marriage. Why would she cheat on him?

"What about Jasen?" I ask.

"I love Jasen, you know that. But things are different with us now."

"Different how?"

"Eleven years is a long time to be married to a man. The passion just… fizzles over time. You get tired of fucking the same guy. I needed to experience someone new. I've developed feelings for Cooper."

I'm quiet as I sip my wine. I know nothing about how passion fizzles over time because I've never been with anyone long enough to find out. My longest relationship lasted a year. And I wouldn't call what we had passionate.

"Jasen is a good guy, Monroe, and you two made a commitment. Are you really willing to risk your marriage for this other guy?"

"Yes. I tried to be a good wife for as long as I could. But I've realized that Jasen and I are not compatible. And you don't know him like I do. He's changed since we got married, and it isn't a good change. I'm tired of being unhappy."

"But Grandma always said that marriage—"

She raises her hand to cut me off. "I know. She said that marriage is sacred, but this isn't the fifties, Mo. I can't take being married to him anymore. I just need a weekend to let loose with Cooper and figure all this shit out."

I had no idea she was this unhappy. But I guess I wouldn't. I tried my best to change the subject whenever she talked about Jasen. When our grandmother died, we were both grieving. We were emotional. She said that her life isn't what I thought it was and she wanted to talk to me about it. But we never got around to it. We had a huge fight over our grandmother's funeral. She wanted to make a spectacle out of it. I wanted it to be peaceful and simple. Just the way Grandma would have wanted it. She called me a tight-ass. She said I was lame and boring. She also said some other hurtful things I'd rather not repeat. Things I thought I could never forgive her for.

Tears form as I think about our grandmother. The woman who raised us. Monroe and I were born two minutes apart. Our mother had gone through a difficult pregnancy and died on the operating table, right after her C-section. We never had a chance to meet our father, who died in an accident four months before we were born. With both of our parents dead, our grandmother felt she had no other choice but to raise us. "Did Grandma Rose know?"

She almost spits out her wine. "Are you kidding me?"

"She gave good advice. I thought maybe you told her that you and Jasen were having problems."

"Hell no. You saw how she acted when I told her I was moving to California with him."

I nod. "She thought you were too young to move across the country."

Monroe's grades were terrible. So bad that she couldn't

graduate unless she completed summer school. After she completed her summer classes, she earned her diploma and followed Jasen to California. We did our best to stay in touch with weekly phone calls that mainly consisted of her raving about how great the West Coast was. She was living free and clear while I was left behind to work and help take care of our grandmother. Jasen started his company, and it took off like wildfire. He became very wealthy, which means that Monroe didn't have to work. She spent her days shopping, soaking up the sun, and drinking smoothies. She was living the life. And she threw it in my face every chance she could get. She offered to fly me to California numerous times, but I declined. I still hated the fact that she had stolen Jasen from me, and I couldn't stand the thought of seeing them together like I had been forced to do in high school.

"Well, I made out just fine. She should have been happy I got out of this dreadful place."

She's making excuses. There was nothing dreadful about the way we were raised. We lived in a middle-class neighborhood of Philadelphia, we attended a decent private school, and we had everything we ever needed. "We had a good upbringing, Monroe."

She shrugs. "Doesn't mean I wanted to spend the rest of my life here. Especially with Grandma Rose and her rules."

"She made rules to make us responsible, but you ignored them every chance you could."

"Are you suggesting I'm not responsible?" she asks, becoming defensive.

That's exactly what I'm suggesting.

"No. I'm not suggesting anything. I'm asking you to reconsider this. It's not every day you marry your dream guy."

"Jasen was never my dream guy, Morgan, he was yours."

I watch my sister's expression change to remorse. "I intentionally flirted with him knowing you liked him."

"So… you never got his number for me, did you?"

"No," she answers.

"I knew it. You tried to make it seem like I was crazy."

"I didn't mean for it to happen that way. I sat next to him at lunch with every intention of telling him about you. But once we started talking, we didn't stop. He offered to take me to a movie, and I agreed without thinking about your feelings."

"I remember that day. I sat in the back of the cafeteria, waiting for the chance to finally tell him I liked him. But then I saw him put his arm around your waist and walk out with you. I knew then he would never know."

Her posture slumps. "I wanted to tell him the truth, sis. I really did."

"Why didn't you? Why would you go out with him knowing what it would do to me? I'm your sister."

"I'm sorry. Please don't think I don't regret what I did to you, because I do. It was stupid of me to hurt you, Mo. I should have told him the truth, but he was a challenge to me. He was the only guy who treated me with respect. All of the other guys just wanted to get inside of my panties."

"Yeah, and you let most of them."

"That's true, but Jasen treated me differently. Which is why I dated him. He actually liked me for *me*, not just my body."

I shake my head in disbelief. "You hurt me, Monroe. I trusted you, and you betrayed me."

Monroe places her glass down and grabs my hands. "I know, and I feel so fucking guilty about it."

"You should. You could have had any guy you wanted. Everyone liked you. I think you wanted to hurt me intentionally."

I see the guilt in her face. The remorse. She nods. "You're right. I did try to hurt you."

"Why?"

"Because I was jealous of you."

"Jealous of me? You were the popular one. I was the weird one."

"But you had the grades. The clean reputation. No one called you *easy* or a *slut*. And you were Grandma Rose's favorite."

"That's no excuse. Sisters don't betray each other like that."

"I know that now. But during that time, I was immature. I lacked self-esteem. And I struggled to fit in, even though I was popular. Morgan. I hate that I hurt you. I'm so sorry."

I'm quiet for a minute as I digest her words. I've been waiting for Monroe to admit that she stole Jasen from me since high school. She flat out refused to own up to it. But hearing her admit it just now and apologize for it finally brings me closure.

"I forgive you," I respond.

"Thank you. I know I should have apologized back then, but I'm glad we're able to talk about it now and put it past us."

I nod. "Me too. And I'm glad you're here. I've missed you," I say as I fight back tears.

Monroe leans in and hugs me. She takes a deep breath and pulls away. "Now, are you gonna help me out or what?"

I take another sip of my wine as I think about my sister's offer. She's serious about this. She wants me to pretend to be her. Deceive her husband. Her eyes are filled with determination. Hope. She's determined to convince me to agree. And hopeful that we can pull it off. I want to say no. I doubt I'll be able to go through with this. And it's wrong on so many levels. But I know my sister. If I don't do this, she'll just find another way to get what she wants. Jasen could find out about her affair. If I agree to help her, I could convince her that she's making a mistake and get her to end things with Cooper before it's too late. It also helps that I'll get to finally see what California is like. I'll get the chance to live in my sister's shoes, if only for a little while. I'll get to feel carefree. I'll get to have some fun. Something I rarely get to do. My days are spent battling an insufficient school system, and my nights are filled drinking wine and reading a good book. I like doing crossword puzzles, scrambles, and playing Candy Crush. It'll be nice to lie out on the beach and relax. Sip some of those smoothies Monroe raves about. Enjoy the nice weather versus the snow here in Philly. For once in my life, I want to break the rules, even though I know it's the wrong thing to do. I finish my drink and watch my sister as she awaits an answer.

"Please, Mo, I need you," she pleads.

"Okay," I agree. "I'll do it."

CHAPTER 2

JASEN

"I thought you were flying back today." I search my desk for the yellow file I need before my client meeting.

"I was, but I changed my mind. I haven't seen my sister in a while, and I need another day to spend with her."

I rub my forehead with frustration. "The same sister you refused to speak to, now all of a sudden you wanna sit around and sing *Kumbaya* with her?"

"She's my twin, Jasen Baker," she states firmly.

"This is the third time you've canceled on me, Monroe. We really needed this getaway."

"I know, but this is important."

"So is our marriage. We never spend any time together. Let alone have sex."

"Is that all you're worried about? Fucking me?" she asks in a low whisper.

I remain silent. It's not *all* I'm worried about. But I was looking forward to being inside my wife this weekend.

She exhales loudly. "I promise I'll make it up to you."

I find the file and fall back into my chair. "I hope it'll be worth it. We need to figure out if we want to make this marriage work or not. I don't know how much longer I can keep doing this."

"Yeah. Me either."

"I'll call you once I land."

"Okay, talk to you soon."

"Okay."

I hang up the phone and buzz Ariel into my office. Ariel is my new assistant. And I can tell that she wants to fuck me. She constantly flirts with me. She brushes her fingers against mine while handing me my coffee, she bats her eyes at me, and she pretends to drop things just so she can bend over. She's been working for me for about three months now, and I know I should have fired her when it first happened, but I desperately needed the help. After my former assistant, Mrs. Gertrude, retired, I had the toughest time finding someone with the right skill set to work for me. And Ariel, as tempting as she is, is a fast learner who hit the ground running. Plus, I've learned how to control the situation. When she makes advances, I quickly remind her that I'm married. Sure, she's attractive. But I won't dare cross the line, no matter how sexually frustrated I am. I take my marriage seriously, and although Monroe can be a piece of work, we've managed to hang in there since the eleventh grade. We're high school sweethearts.

High school was hard for me in California. I was bullied a lot. Teased every single day of the week. It affected my grades and my desire to attend school. When my mother found out I was skipping classes, she thought it would be a good idea to send me to Philadelphia with my father, where I could finish the last few years of school. She thought a change of scenery would do me some good. And she was right. It was something about being the new kid that made everyone curious to get to know me. I was always good at basketball. I played at the neighborhood rec center. But I was too shy to play for the school team. Once I moved to Philly, I tried out for the basketball team, and not only did I make it, I was their star player. I brought the school two championship wins. I was praised. The guys envied me. Wanted to hang around me. And the ladies, they couldn't get enough of me. None of them had any idea of the person I was before I arrived. Shy. Awkward. Misunderstood. I buried that person so far deep that I even forgot who I used to be.

Monroe was one of many girls who took interest in me. But she was the first one who kept my attention. I was drawn to her. I took a few classes with her identical twin sister, and if it wasn't for the fact that their personalities were so different, I wouldn't have been able to tell them apart. Monroe was a firecracker. Still is. Loud and boisterous. Her sister was quiet. But they both were gorgeous. Monroe had a reputation, but I didn't care. She was a challenge for me, and I liked the fact that I was the one who was able to settle her down. Once we started hanging out, we became attached at the hip. After graduation, I decided to move back to California, and I asked her to come with me. She failed her senior year and had to complete summer school, but as soon as she finished, she joined me on the West Coast.

Right after that, my father died, and with the insurance money he left to me, I was able to buy us a small condo. We married at the courthouse a few years later, just the two of us. We struggled at first. I was working for a small security firm that paid me minimum wage, and we all know that minimum wage ain't shit in California. I was barely making ends meet. After two years of subpar bonuses and no raises, a coworker and I decided to quit, and together, we launched our own company, Baker and Tillman. We do it bigger and better. Private investigation. Private security. And some not so legal activities.

We have two offices now and are working on a third. We've beat out the competition, even shutting down the company we used to work for. Life was great. I had job security. Money. And a fine-ass wife who I adored. I was looking forward to having babies. Going on family vacations. I wanted to do what normal married couples did. Save money. Start a family. Plan a future together. At least that was my plan.

But I soon learned that Monroe had other plans. She wants to live like we have no responsibilities. All she's concerned about is shopping and fine dining. She spends thousands a week with her shopping sprees and a few hundred a week dining out. We argue nonstop about her spending habits, and I've had to cut a few of her credit cards. I have money. Lots of it. But I want to save and invest it wisely so I can retire early. Don't get me wrong, I like to spoil my wife. I think she should enjoy nice things. But not every single day of the fucking week. I pay for a housekeeper when I have a wife who is perfectly capable of cleaning up after herself. I cook most nights to cut down our chef bill, even when I'm dead tired after work. And I pay hundreds a week for trips to the nail salon, hair salon, massage parlor, and some steaming place she goes to. Since when do women steam their vaginas? I have no idea what the purpose of it is, especially since I haven't seen my wife's vagina in five months. This is not the life I had planned for us. And I certainly didn't think that my wife would be this way for long. I thought people matured as they aged. But she hasn't. Because of this, we haven't seen eye to eye in a long time. To make matters worse, I'm starting to think that maybe she's having an affair.

My door opens, and in walks Ariel. She's wearing a tight skirt and an even tighter blouse. "Yes, Mr. Baker?"

"Please cancel my wife's flight to Dallas; she won't be joining me after all."

"Maybe I should join you. I'm sure you could use my help," she says seductively.

I rub my chin as I think about her offer. *Don't do it, Jasen. It's not a good idea. Monroe will flip if she finds out you traveled with Ariel.*

"I think you're right. I could use the help."

MONROE

I study my sister through the dressing room mirror of Victoria's Secret. "You've got to look confident, Morgan. You look like you've just seen a ghost."

"I don't wear stuff like this," she answers while crossing her arms. "And how do I even get these strings on?"

"They're not strings, they're straps; it's called a garter belt."

She looks down. "It looks difficult."

"Morgan, part of being sexy is being confident. You already look sexy; you just have to *feel* sexy."

"I hate wearing revealing clothes, let alone lingerie," she complains.

"So, how do you keep it sexy in the bedroom? Wait..." I take a break from connecting the straps to the stockings. "Are you still a virgin?"

Morgan rolls her eyes. "Of course I'm not. I've had sex before."

I continue to connect the straps. "I can't wait to hear about this. There, got it. Now look at yourself."

She looks gorgeous. I just wish I could get her to see it. The outfit I picked out for her fits her body perfectly. She spins around in the mirror and smiles when she comes to a stop.

"You look beautiful, Mo. Jasen will never know the difference."

She stops smiling. "Wait... I thought I was just trying this on. I'm not going to wear this for him, am I? Please tell me you're not asking me to sleep with him, Monroe."

"Calm down. Of course I'm not. You think I would want my husband fucking my twin sister?"

"Then why would I wear this for him?"

"Jasen and I barely have sex. But I like to wear lingerie to bed most nights—it makes me feel sexy. You must do the same in order to pull this off. I wanted you to try some stuff on to boost your confidence."

"I am confident, Monroe. I just don't like wearing these kinds of things. I don't see the point."

I smirk. "You don't see the point because you haven't been with the right man yet. Speaking of right man, who was the lucky guy to pop your cherry? I thought you'd be a virgin forever."

"No one important," she responds.

I don't push the subject; obviously, Morgan doesn't want to discuss the issue. I take one last look in the mirror at my sister and smile. We're definitely going to pull this off.

JASEN

We finally arrive at the hotel, and I'm exhausted from the flight. I'm in Dallas for a business meeting with a potential client who plays for the Dallas Mavericks. He suspects his wife cheats on him when he's on the road for away games but has no way of proving it. His prenup states that she's entitled to half, unless they divorce on grounds of infidelity. So, he needs the proof so he can divorce her while protecting his assets. Monroe was supposed to join me here, and we were going to turn my business trip into a romantic getaway. Instead, I arrived wifeless. I also cut my trip short, opting to fly home right after my meeting tomorrow morning. I miss my wife, and as much as I would like for us to work things out, I'm getting frustrated with the arguing. The silent treatments. The constant excuses whenever I suggest we spend some time together. And I'm extremely frustrated at the lack of intimacy. I can't touch her without her pushing my hand away every time. I'm getting fed up with porn and masturbating. Quite frankly, it's starting to piss me off. I approach the front desk with Ariel right beside me. "Check-in for Mr. Jasen Baker and Ms. Ariel Simmons, please."

The clerk starts to type and then offers me a smile as she slides the key towards me. "You're all set."

I glance down at the key. "You should have two reservations, for two separate rooms."

She frowns as she checks the system again. "I'm sorry. I only see a reservation for one."

I turn to face Ariel. "You reserved *one* room?" I ask.

"Oops," she replies with a smirk.

I take a deep breath as I turn back to face the clerk. "I'm sorry, but we'll need an additional room, please."

She nods as she starts to type again. She stares at the screen for a minute and then looks up at me. "I'm sorry, Mr. Baker, but that was the last room. We're completely booked due to the Cowboys game tonight."

"Then cancel our reservation. We'll find another hotel," I say.

"Sure. But I'm sure they'll all be booked. The Cowboys are playing their rival, and it's a pretty big game. People are here from all over."

I don't give a shit about who the Cowboys are playing. I almost start to tell her this, but I can't take my anger out on her. It isn't her fault. She's just doing her job. This was Ariel's fault, and I will make sure nothing like this *ever* happens again. "Thank you," I reply unhappily.

I walk away, leaving Ariel walking fast behind me trying to keep up. We enter the elevator, and I press the button as the door closes. I'm quiet the entire ride to the eighth floor. I can see her watching me cautiously through the elevator mirror.

The elevator finally dings, and I exit, walking in long strides. I open the door to the suite, but I don't make the effort to hold the door open for her. She rushes in behind me, and as soon as the door slams shut, I let loose. "What the hell was that?"

"What?" she asks as if she has no clue what I'm talking about.

"You know damn well what I'm talking about, Ariel. That fucking stunt you pulled by booking one room."

"They were almost at capacity, and I knew this was an important client. What was I supposed to do?"

"You were supposed to check with me first. You were supposed to let me make the decision. And I guarantee you that decision wouldn't have been the two of us sharing one room. Goddamnit, Ariel! I'm married."

She flops down on the bed. "So, what now? You gonna send me home?" she asks as she crosses her legs slowly.

"No. It's too late for that now. You're already here. I'll need you to take notes during the meeting tomorrow morning and prepare the contract."

She smiles at my statement. "Uh-huh. Jasen, just admit that you're attracted to me."

"You're a beautiful woman—any man would be attracted to you—*but* as I've reminded you on numerous occasions, I'm married. And even if I decided to screw around on my wife, it damn sure wouldn't be with my assistant. You crossed the line."

She stands to her feet and cocks her head to the side. I shouldn't notice, but her nipples peak through the black sundress she's wearing. She watches me with a devious smirk as my eyes roam her body. It's taking everything in me not to turn her around, bend her over the bed, and slide her dress up. I'm sexually frustrated, and being alone in a hotel room with Ariel is not helping my situation at all. Her fingers touch each shoulder, and she slowly slides off each strap of her dress. She allows the top of the dress to fall, revealing her round breasts. I breathe harder as I watch the striptease she's performing. She smiles as she notices the effect she has on me.

"Ariel, I think you need to stop while you're ahead." My tone is far from convincing.

She ignores me and instead, she allows the dress to slide down her body. She steps out of the dress and stands in front of me wearing nothing but red pumps... she hadn't been wearing one single item under that dress.

"Don't worry, Jasen. I'm in a relationship too. This will be our secret, and I promise not to act weird afterwards. Now, are you going to stand there, or are you going to fuck me?"

MORGAN

I fold the piece of lingerie inside of my suitcase as I watch Monroe become agitated with Jasen for not answering his phone.

"He's probably still in the air," I assure her.

"He landed hours ago, and he should have called by now," she says angrily.

"I'm sure he'll call."

"It's not like him to not answer my calls."

I close the suitcase and walk towards her. "Why are you so worried? I'm sure he's okay."

"It seems odd, Mo, and he was pissed with me for not coming with him."

"Why didn't you go? Coming here could have waited."

"No, it couldn't have. We were going to have a romantic getaway to try and rekindle the spark we once had, but I would have been pretending. Coming here was way more important."

"More important than saving your marriage?" I ask.

"Did you hear anything I just said? I don't want to save it. I just want to be with Cooper."

"You won't know unless you try," I respond. "The grass isn't always greener on the other side, Monroe. You owe it to yourself to at least make an effort."

She smirks at me. "Listen to my sister being all philosophical."

I start to laugh. "I've always been philosophical."

"Can't argue with you there," she agrees.

We're interrupted by the sound of a cell phone, and Monroe immediately answers it. I step out of the room to allow her some privacy. I'm having second thoughts about agreeing to switch places with her. Our different personalities concern me. Monroe is fearless, sexy, and confident. I, on the other hand, am shy, distant, and plain. The only thing we have in common is that we look alike. If Jasen were to find out, any hope of reconciliation would be lost, and I want no part in my sister's marriage ending.

Monroe stomps inside of the room, and I immediately know something is wrong.

"What's wrong?" I ask.

"He's lying. I can tell," she answers.

"You don't know that."

"Yes, I do. I asked why it had taken him so long to respond to my calls and texts, and he gave me some bullshit excuse about his phone dying."

"Cell phones die all the time, Monroe."

"Not his. He has, like, three chargers, and one is a wireless one that he can carry around. Work is way too important to him, so his phone is *always* charged."

"So, why would he lie?"

"I don't know, but it better not have anything to do with that bitch Ariel."

"Who's Ariel?" I ask.

"She's his assistant. I noticed her standing a little too close to him when I dropped by the office one evening. Clearly, she was flirting with him, but he denied it."

"So, you think he's having an affair?"

"I don't know, but I'm sure he would if given the opportunity. She's gorgeous."

I bite my bottom lip as my thoughts start to wander.

"What?" she asks.

"It's just… I don't see how you could be upset if he is having an affair. I mean, you're having one."

"I never said I was angry about him having an affair. I said it better not be with *her*. She's his assistant, and it's too risky to mix business with pleasure. We can't have anything ruining the company's reputation or sexual harassment lawsuits messing with our money."

"Oh," I reply softly.

I'm confused. If this is how marriage is, I don't want it. Two people fall in love, only for them to both become unhappy and cheat on each other. Whatever happened to sticking it through and doing whatever was necessary to make it work? Maybe that's why I have such a hard time dating. No one takes relationships seriously anymore.

Monroe plops down on the couch. "I know what you're thinking, and don't worry, all marriages aren't like mine."

"I know. But with my dating track record, I think I'd much rather remain single and save myself the heartache."

"Your Prince Charming is out there, sis. He'll find you. Now, let's finish your 'Becoming Monroe' training. We have an early flight tomorrow, and you have to be ready."

The next morning comes, and I realize this is tougher than I thought. I spent the entire night practicing to be Monroe, and I hated every second of it. As we board the plane headed to Los Angeles, I start to feel butterflies in my stomach, and it isn't from a fear of flying. I'm nervous about what I've agreed to do, and I all of a sudden want to back out. I take my seat next to Monroe and lock my seat belt. She pulls the shade up and stares out her window.

"I think we're making a mistake," I whisper.

"Don't you dare back out on me, Mo. I need you," she replies firmly.

I hesitate as a couple place their bags in the overhead bin and take their seats across from us. I smile at them before I lean in and speak softly to Monroe. "This better just be for the weekend."

"It will be. He's already paid for the Airbnb. We'll be back on Sunday."

"Okay. And you'll call and check on me, right?"

"Yup. Do you remember everything I taught you?"

"Yeah, and I have notes saved in your cell phone. Why couldn't you have gotten an Android?"

"Because iPhones are better. I'm going to hate having this big-ass SG10 of yours for a whole weekend."

"At least mine is more user-friendly," I add.

"You'll get used to my phone once you've used it enough. Now, all we need to do is switch our driver's licenses and our social security cards. Oh, and you'll need my credit cards also. I love to shop, and *you* can't be any different."

"I hate shopping. I usually do it all online."

"Well, that's a no-no, sis. I *never* shop online. Rodeo Drive is the way to go. I like to bounce from store to store."

"I'm nervous," I admit.

"I know, but you'll do great. Think about it, sis, who else would know me better than you?"

I do know my sister well, and I could tell anyone anything they wanted to know about her. But that doesn't mean I want to act like her. Monroe is selfish, conceited, and arrogant at times, and I don't think I can bring myself to act that way.

I place my earbuds in my ears as I rest my head against the

back of my seat. I watch the young kid in front of me stare back and forth between me and Monroe. I smile at his confusion.

"You look like her," he says in amazement.

"She's my twin sister."

"Can people tell you guys apart?"

"Usually no," I answer. And I'm hoping that will be the case this weekend.

CHAPTER 3

MORGAN

"Don't be nervous. You can do this," I repeat to myself at least a dozen times as I walk back and forth in the kitchen of my sister's home.

I had no idea her house would be this big. It's decorated beautifully. It boasts spacious rooms, upgraded appliances, a pool, finished basement, and the shiniest hardwood floors I've ever seen. Monroe gave me the tour of the house, and it had taken me at least a few hours to remember what room was used for what and where everything was located. Jasen would be arriving home soon, and I had to get it together before he walked through that door. Once she was confident that I was okay, she left to meet Cooper. She promised she would stay in contact by text and limited calls, and I would meet her Sunday afternoon at the mall to swap our phones, licenses, and credit cards before I flew back to Philadelphia.

I stop in my tracks as I hear the front door slam. This is it. The plan is in motion. My heart beats faster, and my palms become sweaty as I try my best to remain calm in the denim jean skirt and midriff top that Monroe forced me to change into. I'm sure this is regular attire for her, but it isn't something I would wear, and I feel very exposed at the moment. Jasen walks in with his briefcase, and immediately, my lungs stop working. He drops the briefcase down in front of him and watches me with the sexiest dark brown eyes I've ever seen. This is not the teenaged Jasen I remember. He's bigger. Sexier. His muscles strain against the blue collared shirt he's wearing. His sleeves are rolled up, revealing thick biceps. He looks like walking lust and temptation. He turns and opens a cabinet. "How was Philly?"

"Good," I answer as my body heats from nervousness. And other things.

He closes the cabinet and turns around to face me. He narrows his eyes as he tears the wrapper off the granola bar in his hand. "You're awfully quiet. Is something wrong?" he asks before taking a bite.

"No, everything's fine," I reply.

"How's your sister?"

"She's doing great."

"So, you two are good? You're speaking again now?"

"Yup."

"Good, now you can stop talking about how much you hate her."

"What?" I ask softly.

I'm not sure if I heard him correctly; did he just say that Monroe hated me?

He stops chewing. "Oh, come on, you say it all the time, Monroe. How Morgan was the favorite, and how Grandma Rose always defended her no matter how wrong she was."

So, I had heard him correctly. I'm instantly angered. Monroe hated me. *She* betrayed *me,* so I should be the one hating her, not the other way around. Had I known about this sooner, I would have never agreed to help her. I snap out of it and answer his question. "We worked out our differences. Everything is good now."

He takes the last bite as he watches me. He swallows and tosses the wrapper in the nearby trash bin as he walks closer. My body stiffens when he stops right in front of me.

Uh-oh!

He's entirely too close. His lips are mere inches from mine, and I can smell the mixture of peanut butter and chocolate on his breath. I can also smell his cologne. And it's intoxicating. He places his hand around my waist and gently pulls me to him. "Did you think about my suggestion? Are you willing to try?" he asks.

"Yes," I answer as my eyes fixate on his.

"So, you'll go?" he continues.

"Yes," I answer again, mesmerized by his baritone voice.

"Good. I think it will be good for us," he responds.

He leans in and kisses me, rendering me powerless. My eyes close and my mouth opens as I allow his tongue to enter. Sparks ignite every nerve ending. His hands make their way under my skirt, and he tugs at my thong, pulling it down. It fall to my ankles, and he lifts me up and on top of the countertop. I'm lost in the moment. It's been so long since I've touched a man, and my body is all too welcoming of Jasen's hands. My skirt is lifted around my waist, his fingers are between my legs, and he's kissing my neck softly. "I've missed touching you. I want you so bad, Monroe... right here, right now."

My eyes fly open at the mention of my sister's name, and I clasp my legs together just as his finger reaches my clit.

"What's wrong?" he asks.

"I can't," I answer.

Irritation crosses his face as he reluctantly removes his hand from between my legs. He takes a frustrated deep breath. "What's really going on?"

My mind works overtime trying to come up with a logical

answer to his question. Monroe hadn't given me the details about their sex life other than she was bored with it. I have no idea how frequently they have sex, or if at all. But what he said just now—*I've missed touching you*—leads me to believe she's been holding out. The question is, for how long. "I can't. I have an appointment," I blurt out.

"An appointment?" he repeats.

"Yeah, and I'm already running late."

I gently push him away. He backs up and watches me as I adjust my crop top and fix my hair. I try my best to avoid eye contact with him. He crosses his arms. "You didn't mention having an appointment yesterday," he says accusingly.

"I must have forgotten."

I hop down and balance myself on the wedge heels Monroe suggested I wear. I'm still weak in the knees from the way he kissed me. How the hell could Monroe want to kiss anyone else if Jasen kisses like that?

"Where?"

"Huh?"

"Where? Where's your appointment?"

"At the nail salon."

He glances down at the freshly coated pink polish on my nails. "You go every Monday."

When Monroe dragged me to the hair and nail salon this morning, she failed to mention that little detail. "I don't like the color. I want something different."

He watches me for a minute before he responds, "Okay."

I walk away quickly, eager to get out of here so I can call my sister. I'm drowning here and need help badly.

"Monroe," Jasen calls after me.

I stop in my tracks, but I don't turn around to face him. "Yeah."

"Are you having an affair?" he asks.

I whirl around at his question. He looks pissed, confused,

and hurt all at the same time. I can't leave without reassuring him that he's wrong. I have to make him believe that his wife would never do such a thing, even if it is a lie.

"No. I love you," I say with confidence.

"You love me?" he repeats.

"Yeah," I answer.

"You haven't said that since our wedding day," he responds.

Shit!

This is so much harder than what I expected. I had no idea things were this bad between them. "I'm sorry. I should say it more."

"So, you'll be back in time for the session?" he asks.

"What session?" I respond.

"The session you just agreed to. The marriage counseling appointment I made for us this evening?"

Did you think about my suggestion? Are you willing to try?

So, that's what he was talking about. Nope. I can't do it. I'll crack, I just know it. "Um, is it really necessary?" I ask, hoping to get out of going.

"Very necessary, and you just said yes."

My mind spins with ways to change his mind. If I'd known that this was what he was suggesting, I would have said no. I should have asked questions. Probed further. Instead, I was lost in lust. He senses my hesitation. "Just one session. We'll see how it goes before we make a decision to continue," he reasons.

"Okay. Deal. I'll be back in an hour or so."

"Just an hour this time? You're usually there for at least two."

"It's just a retouch. Shouldn't take that long."

"Okay. But do you have to leave a one-hundred-dollar tip? I'm sure that's above and beyond twenty percent, Monroe."

I nod. "I'll tip modestly."

"Thank you." He grabs his bag off the floor and kisses me on the cheek as he exits the kitchen.

∾

"You can't interrupt me every five minutes, Mo. This is supposed to be my weekend getaway."

"What? This is the first time I've called you since you left."

"I didn't expect to hear from you this soon."

"I bet you didn't, since you hate me and all."

"What?"

"You told Jasen that you hate me?"

She pauses before she answers me. "You know I can't possibly hate you, Morgan. I said that out of anger."

"Okay. If you say so. Listen, I need to ask you something. Why didn't you tell me you and Jasen weren't having sex?"

"I did. I told you things haven't been the same. Why do you think I'm seeing Cooper?"

"How long has it been?"

"I don't know, three or four months maybe. I've lost track. Just say you have a headache if he tries anything. That always does the trick."

I take a deep breath as I drive her cherry-red Range Rover into a strip mall parking lot. I love my sister dearly, but she can be the most self-centered person at times. "Monroe, we're going to marriage counseling this evening. How the hell am I supposed to pull this off?"

"Shit, I forgot he asked about that. I was too distracted to answer him when I was in Philly. Sorry, Mo, I told him I would think about it."

"Yeah, and when he asked me if I had thought about his suggestion, I answered yes without finding out what his suggestion was."

"Why the hell did you do that?"

My mind replays the way Jasen's hands were wrapped around my waist. I can't tell my sister that I agreed because I was melting in his arms at the time. "I thought he would be suspicious, so I agreed," I lie.

"Oh, well, you're going to have to deal with it, Mo. I would've said no."

"Then you should have said no when he asked you. I don't want to deal with this. Counselors can read people. What if they pick up the fact that there's no chemistry between us?"

Another lie. There is chemistry between us. That was just proven when he had his mouth buried in my neck and his hand between my legs.

"Then it would go well. Because that's exactly how things are with us right now. No chemistry."

I exhale loudly.

"You got this, Morgan. It's just for the weekend. I'll be back before you know it to sort all this out."

"Fine. Figure your shit out and return home to your husband so I can get back to my life."

"I will. I gotta go. Cooper and I are about to take a dip in the ocean. I'll text you later, okay?"

"Okay."

JASEN

"I'm telling you, Tillman, she's acting really strange, Something's up." I place my call on speaker so I can unpack while I chat with my business partner. I wouldn't say that we're close friends or anything like that. We have more of a professional relationship. We've hung out occasionally for a beer or two, but that pretty much sums it up. Even then, we didn't share much about our personal lives. He's a very private person, and so am I. This isn't like me to discuss my personal life with him, but I'm desperate for answers.

"You said you guys have been having issues, Jasen. Maybe she's just stressed out about that."

"No, it isn't that. She seems... different. She actually let me kiss her today, and do you know she even told me she loves me?"

"She's your wife. She's supposed to tell you she loves you."

"She hasn't said that since our wedding day. Monroe isn't the lovey-dovey type. She's as tough as nails."

He's only been around Monroe a few times. Once when his wife, Simone, invited us to dinner, and the other time when we invited them to our home. Our dinners were like night and day. Simone made a home-cooked Southern meal. Fried catfish, candied yams, collard greens, and cornbread. I ate until I was stuffed, and afterwards, she presented her famous peach cobbler. Simone showed hospitality. She made our plates and served them to us, she refilled our drinks, she even made to-go bags for us when we left. But what I liked best was the love she showed her husband. She was affectionate with him. Little touches here and there. A peck when they were in passing in the kitchen. She told us about how they met, how it was the best thing that ever happened to her. He watched her tell their story with complete adoration. Things were a little different when we invited them over for dinner at our home. Monroe hired a caterer. Our meal consisted of prime rib, mashed potatoes, and a veggie mix I couldn't identify. We had something called crème brûlée for dessert. The meal was pretty good. But the caterer cost me a small fortune. Monroe wasn't as hospitable. We made our own plates, refilled our own drinks, and there wasn't enough food to offer seconds, let alone a to-go bag. She spent most of the time giving Simone a tour of the house and showing her all the expensive things I've bought her over the years. We didn't share stories about how we met. We didn't talk about our plans to have kids in the future like they did. And when Simone bragged about how much she loved her husband, Monroe just smiled and told her to help herself to more wine. I shake my head and focus on the conversation.

"Maybe she realizes that she's losing you and she's trying to do better. Stop looking at this as a negative," he continues.

I'm quiet as I think about his statement. Maybe he's right. Maybe Monroe is changing for the better. Instead of interpreting too much into it, I should be happy she's making the effort. "I guess you could be right. Maybe I'm overreacting."

"You're always overreacting."

I laugh. "I wouldn't say that. Let's just say I analyze everything. Which is why I'm the best at what I do."

"You mean *we're* the best at what *we* do."

"Yeah, that too. Any plans this weekend with Simone?" I ask.

"Nope, not this weekend. I'm out of town visiting my folks."

"And you left your wife home?"

"Yeah, she decided to sit this one out. She isn't feeling too well."

"Oh, well, send her my best."

"Will do. How about we touch base on Monday to go over the Mavericks case?"

"Sounds like a plan."

"Great, see you then. Listen, man, don't stress too much about the wife. All marriages have issues. Just put in the work, and I'm sure it'll all work out."

"I guess you're right. You give good advice, Cooper Tillman. Thank you."

"You got it, man."

CHAPTER 4

MORGAN

I stare down at my set of freshly painted yellow nails while Jasen drives us. I've been quiet the entire ride as I attempt to settle my nerves. I'm about to speak with a marriage counselor about marital problems with a man I'm technically not married to. What if this backfires on me? I shake away the thought, hoping I have enough strength and deceit to pull this off. We arrive at the building, and Jasen turns the car off. "Thanks for agreeing to this, Monroe."

"Of course," I answer.

"I know you hate this kind of stuff, but I want you to be completely honest with me in there. We can't fix our marriage if we don't work through our problems."

I nod. "Okay. I will."

We exit the car and approach the redbrick building. As we enter, I stop beside Jasen to view the directory. He finds what floor the therapist is on and laces his fingers through mine. "This way."

I follow him down a long hallway until we finally arrive at the office. We approach the receptionist. After he gives her our names, she instructs us to have a seat. My leg bounces with anxiety at what's to come. Unlike Monroe, I'm super emotional. I'm damn near an empath. I take on other people's emotions and feelings, and it drains my energy. What if I become so over-whelmed that I spill the truth to Jasen? It would ruin everything. I'm only doing this to patch things up so when my sister gets back, she can get with the program and fix her marriage.

"Your hand is sweaty," Jasen whispers, interrupting my thoughts.

I still my leg and glance down at our hands, still intertwined. I quickly remove my hand from his. "Sorry."

"Are you nervous?"

"No. Why?"

"Your leg has been shaking like crazy, your hand is sweaty, and… you said you're sorry. You never apologize."

"Yeah, I'm a little nervous."

Before he can reply, we're called to the back. We enter a small and neat office, where we're met by a short middle-aged woman. "I'm Dr. Alana Keith."

She extends her hand to me, but I decline. "Sorry, my hands are sweaty."

She chuckles. "I understand."

She shakes hands with Jasen and offers us a seat on a plush leather couch. She takes the seat in front of us and picks up a pad and pencil from the table next to her.

"Thank you for choosing me as your counselor. My goal is to help you work through your marital issues and remember why you fell in love in the first place. What we discuss in this room is confidential and without judgment."

"Thank you for seeing us, Dr. Keith. You come highly recommended," Jasen responds.

"I believe love conquers all, Mr. Baker. Therefore, I take my job very seriously. Do either of you have any questions before we get started?"

Jasen shakes his head and turns to look at me. "None for me," I answer.

"Okay. Let's get started," she responds.

"Jasen, I'm going to start with you. You're the one who suggested counseling, correct?"

"That's right," he answers.

"Why do you feel it was time to see a marriage counselor?"

"Because our marriage has been in trouble for a long time."

I wonder how long.

"When did you two start having issues?"

He looks over at me, and I shrug. *Hell if I know.*

When I don't reply, he answers for us. "When I started my company. Over five years maybe."

Five years? It's worse than I thought.

Dr. Keith writes something down before she speaks again. "And why do you think you started having problems?

He glances at me again but doesn't answer her.

"Mr. Baker, it's important that you're open and honest for this process to work, even if it will hurt your wife's feelings," she explains.

"When we first got married, it was just her and me in a tiny condo. We were in love. And we made the best of what we had. But once my company took off and the money started rolling in, that's all she seemed to care about."

"You feel she only cares about your money?" Dr. Keith confirms.

"No. I *know* it's all she cares about. As long as she can shop and splurge, she's happy. But it's never enough. I'm married to an ungrateful woman. Nothing I do is ever good enough, and she takes me for granted."

"What does she do to make you feel this way?" Dr. Keith continues.

"I work hard so she doesn't have to work. I give her anything she wants, and all she does is need more... more money, more clothes, the newest car. The list goes on."

"And how does she act when you don't give her what she wants?"

"Like a spoiled brat," he answers.

Jasen looks at me angrily, and my heart stops. He's clearly upset and tired of putting up with Monroe's behavior. I don't blame him one bit, and I'm surprised he's stayed around this long. Damn my sister for putting me in this position.

"Mr. Baker, describe to me exactly how you feel in your marriage."

He continues to watch me as he speaks. "It feels like she only wants me to provide for her, and no matter how much I buy her or how much money I spend on her, it's not enough to keep her happy. We spend no time together. We're not affectionate. We argue like crazy. And we don't have sex."

Dr. Keith writes something down on her notepad, and I sniffle to try and avoid the tears from falling down my cheek. This is what I was afraid of. Becoming emotional. Taking on Jasen's pain. I could kill my sister for this. She has a husband who loves her. A husband who is trying everything possible to save their marriage, while her ungrateful ass is off with Cooper, cheating without an ounce of guilt. My heart breaks for Jasen. I feel no sympathy for my sister.

"Thank you, Mr. Baker. I'm going to ask Mrs. Baker some questions now."

Uh-oh!

"Mrs. Baker, how do you feel after hearing your husband describe his feelings?"

Sad. And guilty for pretending to be Monroe. You see, his real wife is really sleeping with someone else and couldn't give a damn if her marriage was saved or not. Everything Jasen thinks about his wife and marriage is accurate.

"It makes me feel... sorry."

How else can I describe how I'm feeling? I am sorry that my sister is a selfish bitch who is breaking this man's heart.

"Sorry?"

"Yes, I feel sorry. Sorry that he's upset."

She writes something else down. "Just sorry. Are there any other emotions you're feeling?"

I don't answer her right away. I'm too busy trying to figure out the right words to say. If I'm too emotional, it will seem weird because Monroe isn't like that at all. I'm supposed to act like her. Nothing more. Nothing less. But I can't just sit back and allow Jasen to think that she's that coldhearted. That she doesn't love him. I'm sure my sister still loves him. She's just confused right now. She thinks she's happy with this other guy, but I know better. I decide in this moment to be better on behalf of my sister. I say what Monroe *should* say in this situation. Make this marriage better for her for when she returns. I grab his hand. "I'm sorry that I make you feel that way. I'm sorry for hurting you. I want you to know that I do appreciate you and I love you."

Jasen opens his mouth. He closes it. He opens it again. Then he closes it. He's speechless. He watches me suspiciously, and I hold my breath, fearful that I've been busted.

"Jasen, would you like to respond?" asks Dr. Keith.

"I, ahh... it's just... Monroe doesn't apologize, and she hardly ever tells me she loves me. This is the second time today she's said it. I guess I'm just wondering where all this is coming from."

"Mrs. Baker, would you like to answer him?"

I clear my throat as my body temperature rises. The air

becomes thick, and I feel nauseated with the pressure of Monroe's marriage weighing on my own shoulders. "I'm telling you I love you because I want us to work. I was wrong. I should tell you more often how I feel about you, and I shouldn't make you feel as though nothing you do is good enough."

Jasen places his hand over mine. "I've waited a long time to hear you say that."

Dr. Keith seems to be pleased that we've made progress. She smiles as she lowers her head and continues to write her notes. When she's finished, she places the pad and pen on the table next to her. "We're making progress. That means the both of you are dedicated to making your marriage better. I have a few things I want you two to work on once you're home if you're up to it, and if you decide to see me again, we can go from there."

"I'm all for it. What about you, Monroe?" Jasen asks.

I'm sure Monroe would have answered no. She's made it clear that she has no desire to save her marriage, and she seems to think that Cooper is the better man for her. But I can't sit back and watch my sister make a huge mistake. Jasen loves her, but if she doesn't change, I have no doubt he will leave her. So, I give the only logical answer that makes sense. "I'm all in."

MONROE

This romantic getaway is just what I needed. I couldn't stand another minute being around Jasen. Life has become boring with him. It's the same thing every day: he comes home from work, eats dinner, and heads to his office to do more work. Outside of the money, I hate his job. He never tells me who his clients are because of some stupid confidentiality clause in his contracts. What's the fun in being married to a private investigator if he can't tell you who his clients are? He does everything by the book, he's predictable, he's a homebody. I like excitement in my life, spontaneity, and passion. Not predictability and structure. I feel oppressed, like he holds me back from living my life just because he chooses not to enjoy his. He expects me to be the doting housewife, have his dinner ready, keep the house clean, and raise a few kids. Hell no, that's not the life I want, and he knew it before he asked me to marry him. I hate to cook. I hate cleaning. And I never wanted children. He knows the kind of woman I am, and no ring or vow could change that.

Jasen spoils me. He gives me anything I want, and I've always been a priority to him. But things changed some years ago. He started acting all bossy, telling me I need to grow up and be more responsible. He also became overly concerned about our finances. He suddenly wanted us to save more money. He asked me to scale back on my shopping sprees, and he even wanted to downsize the home we live in just because I didn't envision a couple of kids running around in it. "Over my dead body" is what I told him. It isn't my fault that he's so damn frugal. He promised to take care of me when we got married, and I plan to hold him to his word. Besides, we have enough money, so I don't know what the problem is. We can afford for me to shop as much as I want to. I won't stop enjoying my life all because he wants to penny-pinch. It's simple: if he thinks we'll run out of money, then he needs to make more money. Problem solved. I think back to our last argument. It happened a few days before I called Morgan for help.

"You spent fifteen hundred dollars on a bag?"

"It's not just any bag, Jasen; it's a Louis Vuitton."

"I know what the goddamn label is, but that doesn't change the fact that you spent fifteen hundred dollars on a bag, and without my permission."

"I don't need your fucking permission; both of our names are on the credit card."

"Correction, the American Express is mine, Monroe. *You* are just an authorized user, and as of right now, I'm removing you from the account."

"You're going to cancel my card because I decided to treat myself?"

"You call fifteen hundred dollars a treat, yet you have at least a dozen of Louis Vuittons in your closet. Return this one... now."

"I'm not embarrassing myself like that. And besides, I was given a discount."

"I swear to God, if you don't return the bag, Monroe, I will drag you down there myself and make you return it."

The argument ended with me returning the bag, Jasen canceling my card, and me telling him that he can go to hell. Maybe the problems we're facing are payback for me stealing him from Morgan.

I watch Cooper as he gases up the car. Cooper is just as handsome as Jasen. He's tall, with bronze skin and brown eyes. He's physically fit and loaded, just like my husband is. I first met him when I accompanied Jasen to his house for dinner. It was then that I met his wife, Simone. Cooper said she's mentally unstable, although I couldn't tell. I thought she was pretty. Domesticated. But she seemed a little naïve in my opinion. She had no idea that Cooper was gawking at me the entire night. She completely missed the fact that he stared at my tits from across the table. She didn't notice it. And neither did Jasen. They were both oblivious to the fact that we were immediately attracted to each other. It wasn't until Simone served the dessert that he passed me his business card. Jasen was too busy explaining how his mother used to make peach cobbler, and Simone was too busy telling him her recipe.

It started out with phone calls. Then hotel visits. We try to see each other as much as we can. And we're both tired of it. Things have gotten serious between us, so we're using this weekend to decide if we're going to tell our spouses about us.

Or come to grips that this will be the last time we see each other. It's wrong, I know. We're both married and should know better, but we're both also unhappy. Cooper says that Simone throws a rage when she doesn't get her way. He said she's obsessed with accusing him of cheating. Sure, he's cheating on her now, but she was accusing him of seeing other women before me. And he wasn't. He finishes pumping the gas and climbs into the Jeep we rented for the weekend. "Damn, you look beautiful today."

I blush. "Thank you."

"You have no idea how long I've wanted to steal you away for a weekend. You better hope I can let you go after this."

"Are you trying to kidnap me?" I ask jokingly.

He chuckles. "No. Not kidnap you. I'm just trying to make you mine."

My smile disappears at his statement. He can't make me his. Because we both belong to someone else. "How did the call with Jasen go? Does he suspect anything?"

"Nope, just that you were acting weird by telling him that you loved him."

"It's not something I usually say. I probably should have mentioned that to Morgan."

Cooper places his hand over top of mine. "The plan is working, Monroe. He thinks you're acting weird but doesn't have a clue."

"Okay. Well, let's enjoy our weekend, then."

"What if I want it to be longer than a weekend?"

"What do you mean?"

"I mean that I'm not ready to lose you. I know we said we would spend the weekend sorting this shit out, but Monroe... I've never loved a woman in my life the way that I love you."

"What about Jasen and Simone?"

"You said yourself that your marriage is headed for divorce.

Simone knows I haven't been happy in a long time either. We deserve happiness."

"I told my sister it would only be for a weekend."

"Convince her to cover for you a little longer."

"I'm not sure if she will."

He rests his hands at each side of my face. "Monroe, please."

I nod. "Okay, I'll call her."

CHAPTER 5

JASEN

I'm still baffled by Monroe's change in behavior. Apologizing. Telling me she loves me. Admitting fault. To top it off, she changed into a pair of sweats, a T-shirt, and no shoes when we got home. She never walks around barefoot, and she's always dressed in designer clothing. It's like she's changed overnight. It's a good change to say the least. Maybe she does want things to work out between us. I glance at her from across the dinner table. Her head is down as she stabs her fork at the spaghetti noodles.

"Are you okay? You haven't touched your food," I ask.

"I'm not really hungry."

"But my famous spaghetti is your favorite."

"I know. And it's delicious... always. I'm just not hungry."

Part of the assignment that Dr. Keith gave us was to sit down and have dinner together every night. We're supposed to use this time to discuss our day and enjoy some alone time to connect. But my wife seems preoccupied. She's been quiet most of the evening and has barely touched the spaghetti that she usually devours whenever I make my mother's recipe.

"Okay, how about we cut dinner short and take a walk at our favorite place?" I offer.

"That sounds nice. Which place exactly?"

I raise an eyebrow. "The beach where I proposed?"

"Oh, yeah... sure."

I place my fork down and watch her with concern. How could she have forgotten our favorite place? I know we haven't visited in a long time, but she always said it holds a special place in her heart. I'm starting to wonder if therapy was too much for her. Maybe I shouldn't have pushed her to go. But... it worked. She opened up to me. I thought we made progress, but looking at her now, I can tell she's withdrawing again. And it's worrying me. "Are you sure you're okay? Is it something I said to Dr. Keith that has you upset?"

She shakes her head. "No. I'm glad we were able to be honest about our feelings."

She is? So, I was right. Therapy was a good idea.

"But I don't think we need to go back."

"You don't?"

"No. Now that we've been honest with each other, I think we've got it from here."

"I feel like we made a breakthrough. Are you sure you don't want to keep seeing her?"

She nods. "No. I'll do better. I'm going to try harder. I don't need anyone telling me how to do it."

I was right. Therapy has her unsettled. It's why she's been so quiet all evening. The last thing I want is for something else to drive a wedge in between us. "Okay, but if we can't work this out on our own, we're going back."

"Deal. Do you mind if we skip the walk?" she asks.

I hesitate for a moment. "I thought it would be a good way for us to spend time together."

"I know. But how about we hang out on the patio instead, with some wine?"

I see enough of my patio when I'm alone and need to think. I would much rather take a walk on the beach, but marriage is about compromise, which is something she hardly ever does. "Okay. I'll put the food away and clean the kitchen."

"No. I'll do it."

I blink a few times, waiting to see if she's joking. "You'll clean the kitchen?" I ask again for clarity.

"Yes. I said I would try harder, right?"

"Right."

"You go relax on the patio. I'll be out in a bit."

She rises from her chair and starts to clear the table. *Who are you, and what have you done with my wife?*

"How about I help you?"

"Okay."

I grab a pink container that's one of one hundred pieces of an entire collection she purchased last year. She was adamant on throwing this ridiculous Tupperware party just to get people to buy containers and whatnot. A house full of women, wasting money on containers they can buy at the Dollar Tree. But what do I know? I pour her uneaten portion of food inside the container and turn the faucet on. I add the dish detergent before I realize that I've just screwed up in a big way. "Shit," I grumble.

"What's wrong."

"I forgot you hate washing dishes by hand. I'll load the dishwasher for you, unless you want to leave them for Lula in the morning."

"Lula? The housekeeper?"

I narrow my eyes. "Yeah. The housekeeper."

"There's no need to leave them for her. I'll do them. After all, the more housework I do, the more money we save in paying her, right?"

"Right."

"Okay. Then it's settled."

I cross my arms. "Are you sure? I know you hate messing up your manicures."

She chuckles as she crosses the kitchen and stands next to me. "Don't be ridiculous. I can wash them."

Okay, something's up. She doesn't clean... ever.

She immerses her hands inside the water and closes her eyes. "There's something about warm water that is so relaxing."

"Okay. This is weird."

"What?" she asks as she starts to clean the first plate.

"You, washing the dishes. I've never seen you do them."

Her hands stop moving, and a look of worry seems to set in. She bites her bottom lip for a second before smiling at me.

"I meant it when I said I would I do better. I'm not using the dishwasher tonight, Jasen. I'm going to wash the dishes by hand, you're going to finish cleaning off the table, and then we're going to relax on the patio with some good wine and much-needed quality time."

MORGAN

Grandma Rose is probably turning over in her grave.

I dry the last bowl, then pull the stopper out, allowing the water to drain out of the sink. I check the time. I don't want to keep Jasen waiting too long. After he finished cleaning off the table, he grabbed a bottle of wine from the cellar and said he'd wait for me outside on the patio. I shake my head at the thought of Monroe. We grew up with lots of chores. Since when did she become so lazy? She can't do her own dishes? I glance down at the fancy dishwasher located in between the lower cabinets beside me. There are at least twenty different buttons to choose from, and the thought of trying to use it gives me a headache. My cell phone vibrates, and I dry my hands before answering it.

"Hold on," I whisper as I hurry to the guest bathroom. I close the door and have a seat on the edge of the tub.

"How did it go with the therapist?" Monroe asks on the other end of the line.

"How the hell do you think it went?"

"Whoa, what's with the stank attitude, sis?"

"You know damn well why."

"Jesus Christ, Mo, calm down. I just asked how things went."

"Don't call me that, and to answer your question, it was horrible."

"It was that bad?"

"How could you be so cruel and insensitive?"

"What do you mean?"

"You made me believe that Jasen was this bad person. That he was so terrible, there was no way you could be happy with him. Turns out, it's all you, Monroe. You're the reason your marriage is failing."

"That's not true. He's trying to turn me into someone I'm not."

"He's doing everything besides trying to walk on water for you, while you're acting like a selfish bitch. You can't even do your own dishes?"

She chuckles. "No. That's why we have Lula. I should probably mention I don't cook either, so don't go serving full-course meals, Mo. I bring in chefs for that, or Jasen cooks."

"This isn't a joke."

I open the door slightly to make sure Jasen hasn't heard my raised voice.

"Whose side are you on?"

"The *right* side."

"Listen, sis, our marriage was over long before Jasen suggested counseling."

"I didn't know it was this bad between you two."

There's a moment of silence. "Exactly what did he say?" she asks.

"He said you're ungrateful, nothing he ever does is good enough for you, and he wants to fix things with you."

"I don't want to fix anything. I want to be free of him."

"Monroe. Have you even tried?"

"No. Because nothing will fix us. Don't you see that?"

"I can't believe this. Jasen is a good man. You need to get back here and make this right. It's time for you to end this affair with Cooper. Come home, forget about him, and never see him again."

"That's going to be kind of hard."

"What's so hard about it?"

"Cooper is Jasen's business partner. I would end up seeing him at some point or another."

I shut my eyes while I shake my head in disgust. "Out of all the men in California to have an affair with, you choose your husband's business partner?"

"It wasn't intentional, and speaking of Cooper, I need a favor?"

"No more favors," I quickly answer.

"Morgan, I need another week."

"A week?" I almost scream.

"Cooper and I need a little more time together before we return and tell our spouses about us."

"He's married too?"

"Yes, unhappily. Like me."

"Let me get this straight. You're leaving your husband, the man you've been with since high school, to be with his business partner?"

"That pretty much sums it up."

I exhale loudly.

"Please, Morgan. Look at it like a vacation. Take the week to relax and enjoy LA. Take advantage of the house. We have a pool, a Jacuzzi, the works."

"I can't. This is getting too deep, and I won't continue to be a part of this."

She groans. "I guess you're right. I shouldn't have put you in this situation. It's okay if you want to leave. I'll just deal with the aftermath when I get back in a week."

I shoot to my feet. If I leave, Jasen will worry. He will think something happened to his wife. "If I leave, Jasen will worry. He will think his wife just vanished."

"Cooper and I can explain when we get back."

It's a shitty, insensitive plan. The least she could do is let Jasen know that she's okay until she gets back. But she didn't mention that at all in her little scheme.

"That's not how you should—"

I'm interrupted by a loud knock. "Are you okay in there?" Jasen asks through the door.

"I'll be out in a second!" I yell back.

"I can't do this," I whisper into the phone.

"Yes, you can. Just one week."

I close my eyes as my head starts to spin. I could leave and allow Monroe to take care of her own problems. But after spending time with Jasen, I can't just leave him. I would feel horrible. I whisper in the phone, "One week, or I swear I'll tell Jasen everything myself."

I end the call, then exit the bathroom and find Jasen standing in front of the door with his arms crossed. "Who were you talking to?" he asks suspiciously.

"My sister."

"You had to sneak into the bathroom to talk to your sister?"

"I wasn't sneaking."

I walk away with him following me closely. As I enter the living room, he grabs my arm. "Monroe, were you really talking to your sister?"

I snatch my arm away. I'm still pissed about my conversation with Monroe, and right now, he's making me angrier. "I just told you I was."

"I don't believe you. Whoever you were speaking to, you sounded angry."

"I was angry. With her."

He shakes his head. "How are we going to move forward if you're sneaking around? I think you're lying. I think you're seeing someone else."

This gets my attention. I get it now. Monroe hasn't been trustworthy. Actually, I shouldn't use past tense. She *isn't* trustworthy. Jasen isn't stupid like she thinks he is. Because as much as she thought she was sneaking around with Cooper unnoticed, she was wrong. Jasen knows something isn't right. I take a breath to calm myself. "I needed the privacy because she pissed me off. I didn't want you worrying about why I was yelling."

He relaxes his shoulders. "I'm sorry. I don't mean to accuse you, it's just..."

I step a little closer to him. "Don't be sorry. I know I've given you reason to worry, but I want to change that."

He closes the gap between us. "Baby, I want us to get through this."

He leans in and gently places his lips on mine. I can taste the remnants of the spaghetti we were eating earlier. His lips are soft and moist. His tongue slides into my mouth, inviting mine to connect with his. Our tongues meet and reacquaint themselves as his hands find their way to the small of my back. He breaks the kiss and pushes me back towards the oversized couch slowly and carefully.

Oh no!

I can't let this happen. This isn't part of the agreement, and Monroe will kill me if she ever finds out. But as my mind convinces me of every reason why I shouldn't do this, my body is betraying me at the moment. He grabs the corner of my T-shirt and pulls it over my head. I'm not wearing a bra, and my nipples quickly harden from the air-conditioning. He slides my sweats down, and I jiggle out of them, even though I know I shouldn't. He buries his head in the crook of my neck, placing soft and sensual kisses on my collarbone. My head falls back as my nipples become harder. Not from the air-conditioning this time, but from the feel of his lips on my skin. A moan escapes my mouth. His fingers set my skin ablaze as he removes my red lace underwear. He nibbles on my ear before his gaze meets mine. His pupils are darkened. "Don't move."

He stands to his feet and pulls his shirt above his head. Sweet baby Jesus, he has the most amazing chest I've ever seen. I instantly want to rub my hands all over it. He unzips his jeans, slides them down, and steps out of them. He's left wearing a pair of navy boxer briefs that he removes within seconds. He lowers himself between my legs, and they open wide for him. He grinds himself on me. "You have no idea how much I've missed you, baby. Missed this."

He kisses me again, and I lose all sanity. I'm no longer thinking about what's best for my sister. I'm not thinking about the fact that I'm dripping wet all over her husband's dick. And I'm certainly not thinking about the fact that Jasen thinks he's making love to his wife right now. All I'm thinking about right this second is how long it will be before he's inside me. I place my hands on his lower back and pull him closer. He gets the hint and circles my nipple with his tongue before he places himself at my entrance. He slides inside me, and I moan loudly. "That's right. Tell me how good it feels, baby."

I yelp as he pushes deeper. As good as it feels, it's also painful. After all, it's been some time since I've had sex. He stills. "Are you okay?"

I nod. "Don't stop."

He doesn't hesitate. He sinks deeper inside of me, and I welcome all of him.

"Damn, you feel so good," he murmurs.

The pain disappears and is replaced with pure pleasure. I'm overwhelmed with need and intoxicated with desire. Jasen feels *so* good. No. He feels amazing. His strokes are intense. Precise. Hitting every single spot imaginable. "Oh God," I cry out.

"That's it, come for me, baby."

My toes curl, my back arches, and my nails dig into him as I scream out with release.

"I'm coming," Jasen groans right before I can feel him spilling inside of me.

He lies on top of me, and we both breathe hard. He kisses my forehead and watches me tenderly. What I wouldn't give to have a man look at me the way Jasen is looking at me now. What I wouldn't give for sex to be this memorable. I've only been with one man, and he was a selfish lover. I got no pleasure out of it at all. I snap out of my thoughts and realize that Jasen is still inside of me. Guilt creeps in at what we've just done. I crossed the line. I've betrayed my sister. All this time I've spent judging Monroe. I just realized that I'm no better than her.

CHAPTER 6

JASEN

I don't know if I'm losing my mind or if it's the fact that it's been months since I've touched my wife, but for some reason she felt way better than before. I must be going crazy. We've been together since the eleventh grade, so I should know how my own wife feels. But still, there was something different about her just now that I can't quite put my finger on.

I lean in and kiss her tenderly. And she lets me. This is the second time today she's allowed me to do so. Lately, our kisses have been quick and meaningless. They're not filled with emotion, just a peck here and there in passing or when I leave for work in the morning. Monroe isn't fond of kissing; it's too intimate for her. She hates showing any type of emotion or affection, especially during sex. Sex between us involves light touching, no kissing, and no cuddling afterwards. She wasn't always this way. In the beginning, sex between us was amazing and full of passion. But somewhere along the line it changed; she became distant and cold. But just now, she seemed emotionally connected.

I stare into her eyes as I pull my lips from hers slowly. Her face displays worry. "What's wrong?"

"Nothing," she answers quickly.

I ease out of her and stand to my feet. "You're lying."

"No, I'm not. Everything is fine."

I grab my boxer briefs off the floor. "I'm not convinced you're telling me the truth, but I guess that's your answer and you're sticking to it."

She stands to her feet and grabs her clothing off the floor. "Really, I'm okay. I just need a nice, hot shower, that's all."

"Okay, want some company?" Fuck, I hope she says yes so we can have a repeat in the shower.

"I think I'd rather be alone," she replies before leaving the room in a hurry.

I watch her run off with confusion. I don't understand what just happened, or why she's acting strange, especially after the moment we just had. We haven't made love in a long time. What just happened should bring us closer. But it's caused her to run from me. And I don't know why.

MORGAN

How in the hell could I be so stupid? How could I allow myself to sleep with him? Better yet, how could I allow myself to *enjoy* sleeping with him? The minute he pulled out of me, I instantly found myself craving him again. I longed for his body to be pressed against mine, for as long as possible. Which is why I need space right now. I need time to process all of this, and time to calm my raging hormones. I lock myself in the master bathroom, run some bathwater, and pour in some bubble bath. I was going to take a shower, but I think a relaxing hot bath is just what I need right now.

I can't let this happen again.

I find a towel in the closet and place it on a nearby chair.

Once the water reaches my desired level, I step inside of the claw-foot tub and turn the faucet off. As I immerse my body in the water, it instantly soothes me. Just as I relax, the doorknob jiggles, and then there is a knock at the door.

"Monroe, are you okay?" Jasen asks.

"I'm fine," I call out.

"It didn't look like you were fine. You ran off like something was wrong," he continues.

"I'm okay. I'll be out after my bath," I answer, rushing him away.

After a few seconds of silence, he responds, "Okay."

I relax my shoulders and inhale the scent of the jasmine-scented bubble bath. Why did I agree to give Monroe a week? I should have just fled back home and allowed her to clean up her own mess. But for some reason I just can't hurt him. Jasen doesn't belong to me, but I can't bring myself to break his heart.

When I finish cleaning myself, I grab the nearby towel to dry off. I use the almond butter body cream located on the bathroom shelf to moisturize my wrinkled skin. I feel fresh. I smell fresh. And I feel more relaxed. I wrap the towel around me and open the bathroom door slowly. Jasen is sitting up scrolling through his cell phone when I enter the bedroom. His eyes sweep over my body slowly.

"I wanted to talk before we go to bed," he says.

"Okay," I reply as I walk towards the dresser to find a pair of pajamas.

I open the first drawer. It's filled with his boxers.

"Why are you in my boxer drawer?" he asks.

Shit!

I quickly close his drawer and open the one next to it. "I want to sleep in something comfortable tonight," I answer as my eyes land on Monroe's selection of night clothes.

Her selection is little to nothing, just like she said. It's a combination of silk nighties and other identified clothing I've never seen. I grab a pair of brand-new silk lavender panties, rip the tag off, and slide them on before closing the drawer. I open the third drawer, and bingo—I've found what I'm looking for: Jasen's T-shirt drawer. I pull out a gray T-shirt and slide it over my head, then close the drawer and turn around to face him. He looks puzzled.

"What?" I ask as I walk towards the bed.

"You're wearing my T-shirt."

I look down at the shirt. "Is there a problem with me wearing your shirt?"

"No, but you've *never* slept in a T-shirt. You've always slept naked or in some type of sexy nightie."

I'm quiet for a moment as the reality of just how different I am from my sister sets in. I wouldn't be caught dead sleeping in any of the items I saw in her drawer. They're for one purpose only, and once they come off, that's it. I don't know how she's able to sleep in any of that stuff comfortably. "That's the old me, Jasen. The new me plans to switch it up a little. And tonight, I want to sleep in your T-shirt."

"Okay. And for the record, you look just as sexy wearing a T-shirt. I like you in it."

I smile before I slide in under the blanket. "Thank you."

"What happened earlier?"

"I just needed a minute," I answer.

"A minute for what?"

"A minute to myself. To think about everything going on with us. I got emotional."

It's not entirely a lie. I did need a minute to think about everything that's going on with us. He turns on his side and wraps an arm around me. "I know we've been going through a lot. But we haven't connected like that in a long time. I think it's a good thing."

"Me too."

"So, don't run from it. Embrace it. If we're going to fix things, it's important we build our intimacy back."

"Okay." That's all I've got. I'm physically and mentally exhausted. Not to mention the time difference doesn't help. I place my hand over his and feel him kiss my cheek, right before I fall asleep.

MONROE

I roll over to face Cooper, who is sound asleep and snoring. We were up late last night, and I'm sure it will be a while before he wakes up. We spent the evening at a comedy show before heading to a nearby nightclub for drinks and dancing. Jasen would never have agreed to do either of those things. He hates loud music, and he barely drinks. His idea of fun is watching some boring old movie or hiking. Did he really think that I would sleep in the woods, in a tiny-ass tent, and risk being eaten alive by bugs? Absolutely not! I slide out the bed and grab my cell phone off the nightstand. I tiptoe out the room and head towards the kitchen to start a pot of coffee for when Cooper wakes up. I grab a yogurt out of the fridge and have a seat at the kitchen table to dial Morgan. The phone rings twice before she answers.

"How was your first night?"

"Do you even need to ask?"

"Did he try to sleep with you?"

"No."

"Huh, that's unusual."

"We were both mentally exhausted from therapy."

"Ah, that makes sense. You think he suspects anything?"

"No, I'm covering for you just fine."

I let out a deep breath. "Good."

"Are you having a good time?"

"Yes. We're having a great time. Thanks for doing this for me, sis."

"You owe me big-time after this."

"Consider it done."

"Okay. I'll check in later."

"Okay."

MORGAN

I just lied to my sister. But what was I supposed to say? That I screwed her husband and enjoyed every single minute of it? I'll never tell her the truth. The bedroom door opens, and Jasen walks in, dripping sweat and breathing hard. In his hand is a cup carrier with a green drink inside. He hands it over to me. "I cut my run short this morning. Figured I'd pick you up one of those seaweed smoothies you like."

I grab the cup holder and remove the drink. "Thank you." I open the straw and place it inside the cup. I watch Jasen shed his clothes as I take a sip. I immediately gag. He turns around completely naked. "What's wrong? Did they mess up the order? I specifically told them to go light on the chia seeds."

I place the cup holder next to me on the nightstand. "No. I swallowed too fast. It's good, thank you." I take a big gulp, pretending to enjoy it like Monroe would. The disgusting taste consumes my tongue and the back of my throat.

I sit the drink down next to the cup holder and pull the blanket around me tighter. "I was thinking of cooking this morning. I'm in the mood for some bacon."

This conversation is hard to have with him standing in front of me with glistening skin and a perfect physique. "It's been a long time since you cooked breakfast."

I shrug. "Yeah, I know, but that's going to change."

"Did you call Otis to let him know?"

"Yup. Called him this morning."

Of course I didn't call Otis this morning. Because I forgot that my sister has a personal chef to begin with. I make a mental note to call him as soon as Jasen takes his shower.

"Okay. I'm going to shower and head to Mom's afterwards. She wants me to meet her new male friend, who I'm sure I'm going to hate."

This should be music to my ears. Time away from Jasen when I don't have to pretend to be Monroe. Time to relax and turn my brain off for a while. But instead, I'm curious about his mother. I'm curious about his relationship with her. "I'll come with you."

He laughs. "Yeah, right. You hate my mother."

Now I know why Monroe never spoke about gatherings with Jasen's family. Now I know why his mother wasn't at their wedding. She hates his mother. But why? "I don't hate your mother, Jasen."

He folds his arms. "You said she expects you to be a Stepford wife and that you hate being around her."

My heart drops. No. She. Didn't. Monroe was raised to be more respectful than that. "I shouldn't have said that. Please, let me come with you."

He takes a deep breath. "You know how much my mother means to me. I let it slide the last time, but I'm telling you right now, Monroe, you will behave. You will *not* be disrespectful."

I have no words. So, I nod instead.

"Okay. We're leaving at noon."

"Okay."

I wait until the bathroom door closes before releasing the breath I'm holding. I grab Monroe's phone and send a prayer up that she has Otis's name saved. I unlock the phone. Five voicemails. Ten text messages. Three missed calls. I ignore all of them. She can check in with them when she gets back. I scroll through her contacts, and my prayer has been answered. I hit the call button next to Otis's name.

"Good morning, Mrs. Baker."

"Hi, Otis. I'm calling to tell you that you don't need to come and cook breakfast this morning."

"But you requested my special. Bananas Foster french toast."

"I know. I've decided to cook breakfast myself. As a matter of fact, don't come back until further notice."

He gasps. "Are you firing me, Mrs. Baker?"

"No. I..."

There's a moment of silence before he bursts into laughter. "I'm just kidding. Let me know when you need my services, okay?"

I exhale loudly. "I will. Thank you, Otis."

I end the call. And fall back on the bed. Nerves settle in as I think about meeting Jasen's mom. Technically, it's my first time meeting her, and I don't want it to be a disaster. If things don't go well, it could make the dynamic between her and Monroe ten times worse. Maybe I shouldn't have offered to go. I drag myself out of the bed and grab the silk white robe on the back of the door. I slide it on and decide to start making breakfast. But not before I grab the green drink from the nightstand so I can pour it down the kitchen sink.

Spread across the kitchen counter are buttermilk pancakes, perfectly cooked bacon, fried potatoes with onions, scrambled eggs with cheese, and a fruit salad. I'm pouring two glasses of apple juice while Jasen watches with his mouth agape. "Aren't you going to sit down to eat?"

He moves slowly towards the kitchen table. He has a seat and stares down at the plate in front of him. "Wow!"

"What?" I ask as I place our glasses down before taking my seat.

"You haven't cooked for me since we lived in that condo years ago. This looks good, baby."

I smile with satisfaction. "I told you that was changing. I'm going to cook more."

We grab our forks and dig in. Jasen immediately goes for the pancakes, and I can tell by the way he scarfs them down that he's enjoying them. I bite off a piece of bacon as I watch him eat. I feel a sense of pride as he eats my food. I've never cooked for a guy before. "These pancakes taste better than Otis's."

I smile. "They're Grandma Rose's recipe. Thank you."

He places his fork down and grabs my hand. "No. Thank *you*. I know you hate cooking, so this means a lot."

And suddenly, I'm reminded of why I'm here. "I promised you that I would try harder. This is me trying."

"I know I have things I need to work on as well, and I plan on doing my part. Starting with your credit cards. I called the bank this morning and added your authorization back to the American Express card. I had no right to take you off in the first place. What's mine is yours, and I never want you to feel like it isn't."

"You didn't have to do that."

"Yes, I did. It was petty to remove you to begin with. And from now on, I promise to be better with your spending. I'm not your father, and I don't want to act like one. You're an adult, and I have no right tracking what you spend like you're on allowance or something."

I won't spend a dime. Monroe, on the other hand, is going to go crazy when she gets back.

"Thank you."

He smiles before he takes a bite of a strawberry. I continue to eat my food in silence, wondering if I'm making a mistake. Jasen thinks things are going well with his wife. He seems happy. But what's going to happen when Monroe returns and makes it clear that she's not happy at all?

CHAPTER 7

JASEN

We arrive at my mother's house, and I almost vomit when I see her male friend with his arm wrapped around her. He quickly removes it when we enter the living room. "Jasen, honey. You made it."

Her eyes land on Monroe, and she frowns. "Monroe."

"Hi, Mrs. Baker."

My mother hugs me tightly. When she releases me, she kisses me on the cheek. My mother is a beautiful woman. Smooth skin, short curly hair, and a petite frame. "Honey, I'd like you to meet Anthony."

I extend my hand and shake his with a firm grip. "It's nice to meet you."

"Same here. I've heard a lot about you."

I'm being friendly, but my eyes show caution. My grip on his hand says *if you hurt my mother, you'll pay*. He seems to get my point and nods before we break the shake. I turn to Monroe. "This is my wife, Monroe."

He shakes her hand as well, right before we take a seat. Mom sits next to Anthony and twiddles her fingers nervously. She should be nervous. She knows how I am about her dating life. I'm her biggest critic. I immediately start to drill him. "Anthony, where are you from?"

"Born and raised in San Francisco, but I've lived in LA since I was twenty years old."

"Hmmm. What do you do for a living?"

"I sell furniture."

Which means you can't provide for my mother.

"Do you have any kids?"

"Yes, two. A boy and a girl. They're adults now though."

Doesn't matter. I don't want my mother being part of any baby mama drama.

"Ever been married?"

Monroe nudges me. "Jasen," she whispers. She clears her throat. "How did the two of you meet?"

My mom's face lights up before she explains. "I walked into the furniture store looking for a new mattress."

Anthony chimes in. "I knew I had to say something to her the minute she walked through the door."

He grabs her hand and watches her affectionately. But I don't trust him. "And how long have you two been dating?"

Mom looks uncomfortable.

"About six months or so," Anthony blurts out.

"Six months, and you're just now telling me about it?"

The room becomes quiet. I'm seething with anger. How dare she keep this from me? If she plans to have this man in her life, I should have been the first person to know about him. I feel my wife's hand land on my knee softly. "I'm sure she wanted to make sure the relationship was solid before introducing you two. You're important to her, Jasen."

My mother's mouth opens with shock, and so does mine. Did Monroe just speak up for my mother? They've had somewhat of a strained relationship over the years. Mom thinks

Monroe is high-maintenance. She thinks Monroe is self-absorbed and snobby. She's partially right, but I can never tell her that. I refuse to choose between my mother and my wife. The last time I did that, it didn't end so well. Mom invited us to Thanksgiving one year. She asked Monroe to help her in the kitchen, and things went downhill after that. Monroe all but had a heart attack when my mother asked her to help her clean the chicken wings. She refused. She said she doesn't see how someone could touch raw meat like that. When Mom asked how she cleans her meat at home, Monroe dropped the bomb. She told my mother about our housekeeper and that we hire a chef if I decide not to cook. My mother was in disbelief. She couldn't believe that I married a woman like Monroe. A mini argument over domestic duties commenced, and I tried to get between them. Big mistake. Mom didn't speak to me for days, and Monroe didn't speak to me for weeks, each claiming I took the other's side. They don't get along. They avoid each other's presence. But hearing Monroe take up for my mother right now leads me to believe that she has a point. Why else would she defend her if she didn't strongly believe that my mother was looking out for my best interest? "You're right. I'm sorry, Mom. Anthony."

Anthony nods. "I get it. You're protective of your mother. But I'm not here to hurt her. I love her."

Mom stands to her feet. "How about I get us all something to drink? Jasen, I made that homemade strawberry lemonade that you like."

Monroe stands. "I'll help you."

First Monroe cooked me breakfast this morning. Then she defended my mother. Now she's offering to help my mom. She really is making the effort to change. And it's a change for the better. I shake my head and chuckle.

"Everything okay?" Anthony asks.

"Yeah. I think everything's going to be just fine."

MORGAN

I probably shouldn't have interfered just now, but I felt like the situation would escalate if I didn't. Clearly, Anthony and Mrs. Baker love each other. But Jasen can't see it because of his protectiveness of his mother. She's an adult, and he has no right to interfere with her love life. Mrs. Baker opens the refrigerator and pulls out a pitcher of lemonade with fresh strawberries swirling inside.

"Thank you for that."

I grab four glasses form the glass cabinet to my right. "You're welcome."

She places the pitcher on the counter. "Something is different about you."

"Really?"

"Oh, come on, Monroe. Since when do you call me Mrs. Baker? You always call me Charlotte. You're wearing jeans, a T-shirt, and sneakers, for God's sake. I've never seen you in anything but dresses and heels."

I think quick on my feet. "I shouldn't have called you by your first name. I was raised better than that. And as far as the clothes, I wanted to be a little more comfortable today."

Her eyes trail me from head to toe. "Umm hmm."

Here goes nothing. "Mrs. Baker—"

She interrupts me. "I actually like it when you call me by my first name. Mrs. Baker is my mother."

I smile. "Charlotte. I'm sorry for anything I've done or said to you in the past."

She folds her arms and watches me for a second. "You said some pretty hurtful things, Monroe."

I don't doubt that she did.

"I know. And I'm sorry. I really am. Can we start over, please?"

She takes a deep breath. "I'm not exactly innocent in this.

I've done my fair share of being judgmental. But listen, you're married to my son. That makes us family. So yeah, I'd like to start over."

I'm bursting with joy, and I don't know why. When Monroe returns, she'll undo all of this in a matter of seconds. But for now, I have to make it right. It hurts to think that my sister could be so disrespectful to someone's mother. It hurts to know that she caused a wedge between Charlotte and Jasen. I needed to fix this. Even if it's only temporary.

We enjoyed the rest of the day at Charlotte's. Once Jasen was calm enough to let his guard down, he started to like Anthony. They talked about sports, money, and furniture of all things. He also talked Jasen into purchasing a top-of-the-line mattress for our guest bedroom.

Our guest bedroom? Where did that come from?

I quickly remind myself that there is no *our*. There's Jasen and Monroe.

I take a sip of the strawberry lemonade. I'm on my third glass. "Charlotte, this is delicious. Would you mind sharing your recipe?"

She looks over at Jasen. He shrugs. "Sure."

They continue to chat, and I grab my phone to see if I have any missed messages from Monroe. None. I contemplate if I should send her a message telling her that I made peace with Charlotte. But now is not the time.

"How's work going, baby?" Charlotte asks.

"Great. Clients are increasing, and so are our profits. Although, this week will be busier with Cooper being away."

"How is Cooper doing?" she continues.

"He's out of town visiting his mom for the week, so I'll be covering for the both of us."

He's lying. He's with your wife.

"Sounds like you'll have a lot on your plate," Anthony adds.

"Yup, but nothing I can't handle."

Charlotte beams with pride at her son's statement. "You've always been a hard worker."

"I learned from you and Dad."

This is nice. It's been so long since I've been around family that I forgot how much I missed it. Grandma Rose used to host diners for every occasion. Easter, Thanksgiving, Christmas, but none were as important as Sunday dinners after church. She'd invite the entire family over. Hell, she'd invite the entire neighborhood.

"Have you been to see your father?" Charlotte asks.

Jasen shakes his head. "I haven't been to Philly since we buried him."

She smiles. "You should go. And Monroe can see her sister. You have a twin sister, right?"

"Yes, her name is Morgan."

"I'd love to meet her sometime."

I'm unlacing my sneakers when Jasen enters the bedroom. "Thanks for everything today."

I kick them to the side. "I really didn't do anything."

He stops in front of me. "Yes, you did. You calmed me down before I could rip Anthony to shreds. That would *not* have gone well with Mom. And I don't know what you and Mom talked about in the kitchen, but you two seemed to get along afterwards. You guys actually talked."

"We made peace with each other. We both love you and realize we need to settle our differences."

He kneels in front of me. "Good."

His hands slide over my thighs. "It's been a long time since you've worn jeans. These show every single curve."

He reaches for the button. "What... what are you doing?" I ask breathlessly.

He unbuttons them, takes my hands, and pulls me to my feet. Once I'm anchored in front of him, he slides the zipper down. "I'm about to make love to my wife."

He pulls the T-shirt above my head before he kisses me. I wrap my hands around his neck and deepen the kiss, causing him to groan. He breaks the kiss and tugs at my jeans. "Take them off."

I slide out of them quickly and kick them to the side. He nods to my pink boy shorts and matching pink bra. "Lose those too."

He undresses while I slide my panties off and unhook my bra. Moisture pools between my legs at the sight of his naked body. He steps closer. "Get on the bed and spread your legs."

I scoot back on the bed and spread my legs. My eyes trail his as they skim over my body. He drops to his knees and smirks right before he settles his face in between my legs. His tongue rakes over my folds slowly. Oh. My. God. It sends shivers down my spine. My head drops back, and my hand rests on top of his head as he works his tongue like magic.

"Oh God," I cry out.

He works his tongue faster. I grip the sheet with my free hand and scream at the top of my lungs as I come. He softly kisses each inner thigh before he stands up. I scoot back further, and he climbs on the bed and overtop of me. "This isn't going to be gentle, baby. I've wanted you all day. And I need to fuck you right now."

I nod in agreement. I don't care how he fucks me right now. Just that he fucks me. Slow. Fast. Gentle. Hard. Either way, I want it.

CHAPTER 8

MORGAN

It's Monday morning. So, I decide to head to the nearest grocery store. I want to make Jasen lunch and surprise him with it at his office. It's the least I can do since he's working alone this week, compliments of Monroe and Cooper. As I lazily stroll down each aisle, I realize I have no idea what kind of foods Jasen likes to eat. I pull the phone out of my purse and shoot a text to Monroe.

Me: What kind of foods does Jasen like to eat?

I place it back in my purse when a woman approaches me. "Hi, Monroe?"

I plaster on a smile. "Hi."

I have no idea who this woman is, but I fake it, hoping this will be brief. She's beautiful. Golden skin. Slanted eyes. And a body to kill for. She's wearing a white sundress and a pair of green ballet flats.

"I'm surprised to see you here."

"Yeah, I decided to take Jasen lunch today."

"How nice. Well, I'm sure he told you that Cooper is out of

town. I'm just here to pick up some items for dinner for when he gets back."

It's Simone! Cooper's wife.

"Yeah. He did."

There's an awkward silence between us, and I don't know why. Monroe hasn't mentioned any bad blood between her and Cooper's wife. As far she's concerned, Simone doesn't have a clue that the two of them are having an affair. The phone buzzes, interrupting the silence. "Well, it was nice seeing you again."

I reach into my bag as I turn around to walk away. "Monroe?"

I stop in my tracks and turn around to face her. She takes a step forward. "I saw the way you were looking at my husband that night."

I shake my head. "I'm sure you're mistaken."

"No. I'm not mistaken. And I'm not an idiot. I saw you two. Flirting. In *my* home."

I'm stuck. I have nothing to say because Monroe is guilty. For all of it. "Stay away from my husband, Monroe. This is your only warning. Don't speak to him, call him, or go anywhere near him. Otherwise, I'll tell Jasen about the text messages I found in his phone. Do you understand?"

She knows. But most importantly, she's accepting it. Why? Why would a woman decide to hold on to a cheating husband? "Do you understand?" she asks again.

I nod. "Yes."

She straightens her spine. "Good."

She bumps my shoulder with force when she brushes past me. I pull the phone out of my purse to read Monroe's reply.

Monroe: You don't need to worry about that. Jasen does the cooking or we call our chef.

She's useless. And I don't want to press the issue because then she'll have questions about why I'm making him lunch.

And I'll have to lie to her... again. Seems that's the norm between her and me lately. My fingers hover over the screen, debating if I should tell her about my encounter with Simone. Maybe if I tell her that Simone knows and has threatened to tell Jasen, it'll cut their trip short. But knowing my sister, I doubt it. She does things when and how she wants to. Not at any anyone else's pace.

Me: Okay.

After sending my reply, I decide to make something simple. Something I'm sure he's had before. Especially during his time in Philadelphia. A hoagie. I grab ham, capicola, salami, provolone, pickles, peppers, seasonings, and oil. I stare inside of the cart to make sure I haven't forgotten anything when the phone rings. It's Monroe.

"Hey."

"Why do you need to know what foods Jasen likes?"

"I was thinking of cooking dinner."

"But I told you I don't cook. Why the hell would you do that?"

I'm silent.

"Morgan, what is this all about?"

I honestly don't know.

"Nothing. I just wanted to do something nice, that's all."

"You're not there to do anything nice. Especially considering it's not something I would do."

"Okay. You're right."

"Morgan. Is there something going on? Anything you need to tell me?"

"Don't be ridiculous. Of course there isn't."

There's a moment of silence. "Okay."

"I've got this under control. Go have fun."

"Thank you. I knew you wouldn't let me down."

JASEN

Ariel enters my office. "You wanted to see me?"

"Yes. We got the account."

"That's great news. No way he could turn us down after our pitch."

"Do you have the contract ready?"

"Done. Already completed and ready to email."

"Great. I'll need you to contact Roberto. Get him to hack the wife's cell phone and pull the records."

"Do you think she's really cheating?"

"I don't know. But we're about to find out."

She nods. "I'll go email the contract."

She turns on her heels, but I stop her. I've been dying to talk to her about Dallas. "Ariel."

She spins around. "Yes."

"About Dallas."

"What about Dallas?" she asks.

"It can never happen again."

She walks towards me and stops in front of my desk. "Relax. It won't."

"I don't want things to be awkward between us. It's important we remain professional."

"I agree," she responds.

She bends over and slides her hand over top of mine. "I like you, Jasen, but I don't want to complicate things and lose my job."

"I'm glad to hear that."

We're interrupted by the sound of someone clearing their throat. I look up and see my wife standing in the doorway with a basket. I stand. "Hey, I didn't know you were dropping by."

She's dressed differently today. But damn, she looks sexy. The denim jean dress, she's wearing stops at her knees and hugs her hips, and the yellow heels make her look taller. Her hair is tied in a bun, and she's not wearing any makeup. I forgot just how beautiful she looks without all the extras. But she's been doing a good job of reminding me lately. I walk around my desk, cross the room, and kiss her on the cheek.

She glares at Ariel. This isn't good. Monroe has a temper. A bad one. The tension is so thick you could cut it with a knife. If I don't do something fast, this day will end with Ariel lying on the floor and my wife needing bail money.

Monroe frowns. "I thought I'd surprise you. Bring you lunch today."

"I'll send the contract, Mr. Baker. It's nice to see you again, Mrs. Baker," Ariel says on her way out the door.

Once the door is closed, Monroe walks towards the conference table I use for my meetings. She's quiet as she places the basket on the edge of the table. She's pissed. Monroe is never quiet, so either she's thinking of a way to kill me, or this is the calm before the storm. I approach her carefully, hoping I can explain that what she just witnessed is not as bad as it probably looked. Who am I kidding? It's exactly as bad as it looks. Ariel had her hand covering mine. How the hell do I explain that?

"What was that all about?" she asks as she turns to face me.

"It's not what you think."

"I think it's exactly what I think. I saw it with my own eyes. Your coworker holding your hand?"

Anxiety creeps in, and I take a deep breath. She's right. She did see what she thought she saw. Only I didn't initiate it. Not that it matters. I'm going to have to come clean with her about Ariel. It's not the first time she questioned our relationship. She dropped by the office unannounced one evening just as Ariel was about to try and kiss me. I brushed it off like it was nothing. I told her she was overreacting and had no reason to worry about Ariel. I lied. I lied because we were having issues and I was tired of arguing. I lied because I knew if she knew the truth, she wouldn't want me to continue working with Ariel. But it's time I come clean. "Let's sit and talk."

We take our seats. I loosen my tie as she opens the basket and pulls the items out. She's made hoagies, one of my favorites. She also has chocolate chip cookies that look homemade, and potato chips. I tap my finger on the table as she places two water bottles down. The bottles aren't filled with water. They're filled with Mom's famous strawberry lemonade. When everything is spread on the table, she folds her arms. "Go ahead, start talking."

I take a deep breath. It's time I get this over with and deal with the consequences. "You're not going to like what I have to say, but I want to be honest with you."

"Okay, then be honest."

"When you changed your mind about coming to Dallas with me, Ariel traveled with me instead."

She watches me intensely, allowing me to continue.

"And, ah…"

"And what?" she asks.

"And… we almost slept together."

MORGAN

I knew that was the tramp my sister had been worried about. Monroe had been right with her suspicions. Ariel did travel to Dallas with Jasen and was most likely the reason he wasn't returning her calls that day. I wanted to surprise him today. Wear something sexy for him. The dress I'm wearing covers more than what Monroe would cover, but I feel sexy in it. And what I'm wearing underneath it—my sister was right. Wearing sexy undergarments does make me feel confident and sexy. I smiled as I approached his office, but that smile soon disappeared when I caught Jasen and his assistant extremely close to one another. I can't explain it. But when I saw the two of them together, I became jealous. Even though I shouldn't be. Maybe it's the whole twin-empathy thing. No. That can't be it. Because Monroe didn't care if he was having an affair. She only cared about the effect the affair would have on his reputation and business. So then why am I jealous? It's a question I can't answer right now. All I know right now is that Ariel is a homewrecker, and I don't like this one bit. Whatever it is that's going on between them, I'm putting a stop to it right this minute.

"How the hell do you *almost* sleep with someone?"

"She came on to me. I had a weak moment, but I didn't go through with it."

"Oh yeah. So, tell me, what *did* you do?"

I can't say exactly how Monroe would react in this moment. But I have a feeling she probably would have punched Ariel in the face and slapped Jasen. She would have caused a whole scene. I don't feel right doing any of that. Why? Because one, I'm not her. And two, because Jasen is being honest. And that's more than what I can say about Monroe. If this were Monroe sitting here instead of me, there wouldn't be shit she could say to Jasen, after what she's done. He shifts in his seat uncomfortably before he responds. "You really want to know?"

"Do you want us to be able to move past this?"

"Yes."

"Then I need to know."

He stares at me for a minute before he leans back in his seat. "Okay, then. I asked her to join me because I needed her at the client meeting. When we arrived at the hotel, I found out that she booked one room for the both of us. I wasn't happy, but there was nothing I could do at the time because all the nearby hotels were booked due to the Cowboys game."

"There is something you could have done. You could have called me to let me know."

"You're right." He pauses for a moment. "When we got upstairs to the room, I yelled at her. I told her that what she did was unprofessional, and I reminded her that I'm married. She didn't care. She took off her clothes and made it clear that she wanted to fuck me. For a moment, I got weak. I kissed her."

There's that feeling of jealousy again.

"But then I snapped out of it and realized what I was doing," he continues. "I swear that's all that happened."

"And what happened after that?"

"I pushed her away. I told her it was a mistake. My client has connections at the Marriott. One phone call, and he was able to get me a room there. Ariel and I slept in two different hotels. We met at the airport that morning, and I came straight home."

I don't know how to respond to him. On one hand, I think it speaks volumes that he came clean about it. But on the other hand, would he have done so if I hadn't walked in just now? Was Monroe right? Is he just as much to blame for their marriage problems as she is?

"Baby. Please say something."

"Why?"

The damage is done. But I need an explanation. I need to know why he did it. "Why?"

"Yeah. Why did you kiss her? Are you attracted to her? Do you want to sleep with her?"

He shakes his head. "You don't want the answer to that."

"Yes, I do."

"She's been coming on to me since she started. I've always turned her down. I've always reminded her that I'm married. That we need to keep it professional." He stops talking and looks me in the eyes. "It had been months since you let me touch you. You made me feel unwanted. In that moment with her, she made me feel wanted. And against my better judgment, I *almost* did something I know for sure I would have regretted."

His answer doesn't make me feel any better. He had no right being alone in a hotel room with Ariel in the first place. Especially knowing how Monroe would feel about it. He had no right to touch her, knowing he had a wife back at home. But I understand his reasoning.

"I made a mistake. I'm sorry. And it'll never happen again."

"I want her fired."

The words blurt out naturally. I'm not comfortable with him working with a woman he kissed. I mean, Monroe wouldn't be comfortable. She wouldn't like this. And I'm sure she would agree that firing Ariel is the best course of action right now. He looks surprised. "That's a bit extreme, don't you think?"

"No. I want you to fire her... today."

"Monroe, do you have any idea how hard it was to find good help after Gertrude retired? Ariel is good at what she does. I made it clear that what happened was wrong and nothing like that will happen again."

"What she does is seduce married men. I'm supposed to be okay with you working with her after this?"

He rubs his face in frustration. Clearly, he's not happy about my suggestion. "No. You're right. I shouldn't have put you in this position, and now I'll do whatever I have to do to fix it."

"Good. Let's eat."

He raises an eyebrow. "That's it?"

"What?"

"I thought by now you would have set the place on fire."

Monroe would have.

"I'm working on my temper. And if we're going to work this out, we need to be able to admit our faults, come to a resolution, and move past it."

He grabs his hoagie. "Okay."

I take a bite of my hoagie. As we eat in silence, my mind drifts to Monroe. Should I tell her about this? That seems to be a recurring question lately.

"This is nice," Jasen says, interrupting my thoughts.

"What?"

"You surprising me with lunch. It means a lot. Thank you."

"You're welcome. Do you like the sandwich?"

"I love it. We should do lunch together more often."

"I agree."

He reaches over and grabs my hand. "I'm glad you came today."

His eyes show adoration. His touch makes my insides warm and fuzzy. I've never had a man look at me the way he does. Care for me. Want me.

Careful, Morgan. He doesn't belong to you.

"I'm glad I came too."

"And I promise. No more secrets."

But I'll have one.

"No secrets."

He stands to his feet and walks around to my side of the table. He takes my hand and pulls me up in an embrace. "I love you."

He kisses me. His lips are twangy from the pickles in the hoagie. But I don't care. My knees become weak, and my legs clench together as he kisses me deeper. I want him. Here in his office. I shouldn't want to do it. But I do. I've spent less than a week with Jasen, but I find myself comfortable around him. I can be myself. There's a sense of calm and peace when he's near me. And the attraction... every time I look at him, I want him to undress me. I don't know what has come over me. I don't know who I've become. But I don't take the time to think about it right now. I start to unbutton his shirt, but he stops me. "Wait, let me lock the door."

JASEN

After I lock my office door, I walk over to my desk and press the button located under it that automatically closes the drapes. I don't need all of Los Angeles seeing what I'm about to do to my wife, and I certainly don't want anyone else seeing her naked except for me.

"Come here," I order, eager to have her close to me.

She walks towards me nervously, as if she's unsure about what we're about to do. What I'm about to do to her shouldn't be a surprise. I used to make love to her in my office all the time. When she reaches me, I slide my hands to her back and unzip the denim jean dress she's wearing. She slides it down her body, shimmying out of it. When she steps out of her dress, I almost come on the spot. She's wearing a white strapless bra and the tiniest white G-string I've ever seen. Typical of my wife. I take a step back and unbutton my shirt. I nod towards her G-string. "Spin around so I can see. Slowly."

She spins around seductively. And by the time I'm fully undressed, I'm rock hard. "You wore those for me?" I grab my swollen dick. "You wanted this, didn't you?"

"Yes."

She unhooks her bra and tosses it behind her, and then she slowly slides her G-string down. When she steps out of it, she closes the gap between us. In one swift move, I lay her on her back. Thank God I put everything away this morning. My desk is clean, clear, and ready to be saturated with her juices. I take a minute to admire her. Spread out on my desk, waiting for me. Her body is perfect. Always has been. Damn, I've missed her. I kiss her neck while my hand slides down her thigh and between her legs. I circle my tongue around her nipple, and maybe it's just me, but it tastes as sweet as honey. She gasps when my fingers tease her. "You're dripping."

She replies by pushing herself towards my fingers. And when my finger reaches her swollen bud, she moans loudly. I place a hand over her mouth. "Shh, someone might hear you."

Her heavy eyes meet mine. She's wiggling underneath me and moaning loudly underneath my hand. My stare grows intense. I know she's close. I remove my hand and place my mouth next to her ear. "Come for me."

She grabs a hold of me and bites down on my shoulder to muffle her scream. Her juices trickle down my hand. This is erotic at its best. I nudge her legs open and slide in with ease. I pause. There's no way she can feel this good. But after the first stroke, I'm proven wrong. Because she does feel *that* good. She holds on to me tightly as I stroke her. The desk rattles underneath us. It's only been a few minutes, but it's all too overwhelming. Her moans. The scent of her consuming my office. The way she fits me like a glove. "I might not last, baby." I'm a man. I have pride. You could even say I have an ego. So, of course I try my best to last as long as I can. After all, it's my duty to make sure her pleasure comes before mine. But at the rate things are going, I'm not sure I'll be able to do so.

Her moans become louder. She squeezes me harder. "Oh... Jasen!"

I feel her pulsate around me, and my ego goes out the window. Along with my pride. I come. Hard.

We stay in position for a few minutes. I remove the strands of hair stuck to her face. "You are by far the most beautiful woman I've ever laid eyes on."

I kiss her one last time before I pull out of her. I walk into my bathroom, grab a towel, and hand it to her. I watch as she cleans herself. Suddenly, I don't want her to leave. I want to go home with her. Spend the day with her in bed. But I have an important meeting I can't miss. "I have a meeting this afternoon. How about afterwards, I take you shopping? Get you that Louis Vuitton bag I made you return, or anything else you want."

She doesn't look as happy about the idea as I thought she would, but she agrees. "Sure."

CHAPTER 9

MORGAN

My eyes almost bulge out of my head at the prices I'm seeing. Jasen got home around three, and we decided to go to Rodeo Drive and some other expensive mall he wanted to take me to. The average piece of clothing is over five hundred dollars, and that's for a T-shirt. *A freaking T-shirt!* The shoes are over a thousand dollars a pair. And the jewelry is especially expensive. The stuff isn't even all that nice. I've seen better designs at H&M and Fashion Nova. I'm out of my element here. But Jasen thinks this makes me happy. So, I go along with it.

"That'll look good on you," he says as he observes me holding the beige Burberry trench coat.

I grab the price tag and almost choke. "It's over four thousand dollars."

"And? That's less than the two you have in the closet now."

I place the coat back on the rack. I can't take this anymore. I'm about to lose my mind. Monroe really had it good. While I was back in Philly, struggling to make ends meet, she was buying designer things. And she wants to give it all up. Or maybe she doesn't. Maybe Cooper buys her whatever she want's just like Jasen does. "Did you hear me?" Jasen asks, interrupting my thoughts.

"No. I'm sorry."

"I said get the coat."

"No. Like you said, I already have a few. I was just browsing."

"Okay. So, where to next?"

I don't want to be here. Monroe said she shops a lot. She said that I can't be any different. But I can't bring myself to do it. The thought of buying any of these expensive things makes me nauseous. I won't force myself to do this. "Let's go to the nearest antique store?"

He looks at me like I've grown two heads. "Antique store?"

"Yeah."

He crosses his arms. "Monroe, I don't think you've ever set foot in an antique store in your life. You hate those places."

She used to love them when we were kids.

"I know, but I want to do something different for a change."

He looks around the store reluctantly. "Are you sure?"

"I'm positive."

Now, *this* is more up my alley. As I stroll through each aisle of the antique store, a feeling of nostalgia sweeps over me. It reminds me of Grandma Rose. Of home. She used to drag us to these places all the time as kids. I hated it at the time. I hated waiting for hours while she picked up knickknacks and old albums. I thought these places were for old people. After all, those were the only ones shopping there. And it smelled funny. Monroe loved to go. Not because she enjoyed antique items. Because she liked to get into trouble. She would run through aisles and hide. She would knock things over, blaming it on ghosts. She picked up everything, even though Grandma

Rose said no touching. It wasn't until Grandma Rose died that I saw the treasure in antique stores. I would go as a reminder of her on days when I missed her the most. Every item has a story, and I would spend hours dreaming of what those stories were.

"You know, I thought you were joking when you said you wanted to come here."

"Nope. I actually like antique stores."

"Since when?"

"Grandma Rose used to take us." If Monroe doesn't want to tell him, I'll tell him for her.

"I know you must miss her. Even though you barely talk about her."

"Yeah. I do."

"So do I. She was like a grandmother to me."

She was. Grandma Rose adored Jasen. She thought he was the perfect gentleman. And right for Monroe. But she didn't necessarily think Monroe was right for him. She used to say it all the time. Monroe was too fast for any man worth having. I spot an old typewriter and rush towards it. "I've always wanted one of these."

Jasen watches me with confusion. "You have?"

I don't write. But I like the way they look. I've always wanted one just to have for decoration, as bad as that sounds. I check the price tag and smile. "This. This is what I want."

He chuckles. But when he sees I'm not laughing, his expression grows serious. "You want this. Not a pair of designer shoes. Or a designer bag. But... this?"

I grab his hand. "You said I can have anything I want. Well, this is what I want."

$\sim$

I wipe the sour cream from the corner of my mouth as I watch Jasen struggle with his overstuffed taco. "I told you, you added too many toppings."

He takes a bite before it crumbles apart. "You can never have too many toppings," he responds after he swallows.

I shake my head. "You've got way too much guacamole."

He looks down at it. "This is fresh guacamole. I don't think I have enough."

After we left the antique shop, I got hungry. I saw this taco spot on the way home and suggested we stop here. His expression was priceless. He looks around the place. "You know, I like this."

"Like what?"

"Everything about today. Having lunch together, shopping at the antique store, and sitting here eating messy tacos. I like this new version of us. The new version of you."

"What version is that?"

"You seem... carefree. You're dressing more comfortably. You're no longer allowing money to define you. Or labels. Or status. You seem happy with me today, no matter what we were doing."

"That's because I was."

The plan has failed. I was supposed to pretend to be Monroe. I was supposed to do all the things she likes to do. Wear the things she likes to wear. I haven't done that at all. I've worn my own clothing. I haven't worn much lingerie for Jasen, besides a few pair of sexy panties. They do the job, but they're nothing compared to what I saw in her drawer that night. I don't talk like her at all. I can't speak with such narcissism and disrespect. And instead of giving Jasen the impression that I've given up on the marriage, I've done the opposite. I've made things better. Made him believe the marriage is worth saving and that Monroe is doing everything possible to work things out. I've shown him a different side of his wife. A side he never knew existed. What's going to happen when Monroe returns? What's going to happen when she drops the bomb that she's leaving him for Cooper? How is Jasen going to feel when she tells him that she no longer loves him? I didn't think about this when I decided to be myself. I was too busy enjoying Jasen's attention, wishing it was for me to keep. I know my sister. And no matter how much I convince her otherwise, she's got her mind made up. She doesn't realize what she has is special. Does she realize how many women would give their right arm to have a husband like Jasen? Including myself. I shake my head at the thought. It's only been a few days, but I'm getting in too deep. I can feel it. I can feel myself wishing I were her. For the first time in my life, I'm living. I'm happy. I know what it feels like to have a man love me. Really love me. And although I know that this will all end in a week, I really wish it didn't have to.

JASEN

Last night was the most fun Monroe and I have had in a long time. It felt like we were teenagers again. Just hanging out. Enjoying each other's company and eating whatever we could afford. Long before we could afford shopping sprees and expensive restaurants. It felt carefree. Genuine. I never stopped loving my wife. But yesterday, I found myself falling in love with her all over again. She said she would try, and damn if she hasn't stuck to her word.

I exhale loudly as I'm knee-deep in files right now. Since I had to fire Ariel yesterday, I'm currently on the hunt for a new assistant. And it's not going so well. I have no idea where she kept my schedule, the phone is ringing off the hook, and I'm pretty sure I broke the coffee machine this morning. I have three other employees here. Sean, my accountant. Silvia in IT, who is out on maternity leave. And Jake, the janitor. None of them are of any help to me right now. I find the file I think I'm looking for and open it with hope. "Damn it!"

"Everything okay?" Monroe asks from my doorway.

This is the second time she's visited me in the office this week. And just like yesterday, she looks good enough to eat. She's wearing a black pencil skirt, a pink blouse, and a pair of pumps. Her hair is in a braid on the side. She's dressed like she wants to role-play. Student/teacher, or boss/employee. And as much as I would like to take her up on her offer, I can't. I'm way too busy. "Hey."

"You look busy."

"I'm swamped. With Cooper out of town and Ariel gone, I'm losing my mind. Sorry, sweetheart, I'd love to have lunch with you again today, but I just don't have the time to eat right now." I stop what I'm doing and drag my eyes from her head to her toe. "Even though I'd love to rip that skirt off you right now and have a taste."

She shakes her head as she walks towards me. "I'm not here for lunch today."

This catches my attention. "Is something wrong?"

"No. I'm here to help you."

"Help me?"

"Yeah. I know you thought Ariel was good help, but I can be just as good. I'll help you until you hire a new assistant."

I'm now convinced that Monroe is using drugs. Or has had a mental breakdown. No way in hell would she suggest helping me. She hates working. "Are you being serious, honey? Because now is not the time to joke about—"

She cuts me off. "I'm serious, Jasen."

"Okay. Am I paying you for your services?"

She giggles as she turns to walk away. "We'll figure something out."

An hour later, Monroe pokes her head in my office. "You have a conference call at two o'clock with a Sally Arden."

"Shit, I don't know where Ariel kept her file."

She walks over to my desk and leans over me. She clicks something on the screen, and the image of a folder pops up. "I'm scanning all of your files electronically. This way, you can find a file with the click of a button. Sally's file was scanned in this morning."

I look closer at the screen. Everything is there. She's even filed it by last name. "Well, I'll be damned. How come Ariel never thought of this?"

"Because she wasn't as good as you thought she was."

She's clicking on something else to show me. But I'm too busy inhaling her perfume and staring at her tits to notice. "Jasen, pay attention."

"I'm sorry, sweetheart. But damn, you look sexy today."

She swats me on the shoulder. "I'm here to help you. Professionally."

I turn my focus to the screen. "Okay."

"This is your calendar. I linked it to your email, so you'll get notifications fifteen minutes before your conference calls and a day before your meetings. For your out-of-town meetings, you'll get the notification a week before."

I'm in awe. "How did you learn to do all of this?"

She pauses for a second. "I, ahh, I had a clerical job in high school."

"I don't remember you working when we were in high school."

"It was before I met you."

"I'm impressed, baby. You've been a big help today. Thank you."

"You're welcome."

"How about I take you to dinner tonight as a way of saying thank you?"

She places her hand on her hip. "Are you asking your assistant on a date, Mr. Baker?" she asks seductively.

So, she does want to role-play.

"I am. And I hope she says yes."

She turns on her heels and sashays slowly towards the door. She stops when she reaches it. "I'd love to. I'll be at my desk, if you need me."

MORGAN

I felt a little guilty making Jasen fire Ariel. So, I stopped by the office and offered to help him. I wasn't sure if he would agree or not, but I'm glad he did. I settled into the desk that Ariel occupied nicely. After I tossed out the items she failed to take with her, I got the phone number for Sylvia, Jasen's IT person, and she helped me bypass Ariel's locked screen on the computer. She set me up with my own username and password, and she gave me access to Ariel's emails and files so I could pick up where she left off. I was right. Once I logged in, I no longer felt guilty for asking Jasen to fire her. She wasn't as good as he thought she was. Jasen's files were a mess. They were unorganized. The physical files had paper sticking out of them instead of being clipped and secured tightly inside. And to make matters worse, the notes she took from meetings were all done by hand. And her handwriting was worse than a two-year-old's. Jasen would never be able to go back and understand what she wrote. I spent most of the morning scanning all the files electronically so that he could access them with a click of a button. It'll take me weeks to get him organized and up and running efficiently. Weeks that I don't have.

I rushed home around three o'clock. I was expecting to make it home in an hour, but I was quite surprised at the amount of LA traffic. The GPS took me on a detour, and I didn't make it home until well after five. No wonder Monroe suggested I Uber instead. Speaking of Monroe, I haven't heard from her. And some small piece of me is okay with that.

I've spent the past few hours rummaging through her closet when I receive a text from Jasen.

Jasen: I've made reservations. Wear something sexy.

Me: Can't wait.

I grow excited, wondering where he's made reservations to. Almost like a first date. I pause. It isn't right to feel this way. I've crossed the line so many times in this situation, and it could cost me my relationship with my sister. I could argue that she's the one who put me in this situation. I could argue that she's the one having the affair. But I would still be wrong for what I've done. I dial her number. It rings and rings until her voicemail picks up. I leave a message.

"Hey. I haven't heard from you. I know you said not to bother you, but I wanted to check in and see how things are going. Call me back. Bye."

My eyes land on a black satin dress. I slide it off the hanger. It's beautiful. Simple, classy, yet sexy. It's perfect for tonight.

After my long shower, I take the time to apply some light makeup, just like Monroe taught me to. I've only worn it a few times in my life. My senior prom, where I attended solo and spent the night watching Monroe and Jasen have the time of their lives. And at our great-aunt's wedding. Back then, makeup was different. It was bolder. Brighter. Monroe showed me how to give myself a softer look, with natural colors. After I'm done, I sweep my curled locks into a messy bun and put on a pair of diamond studs. There's a knock at the door.

"Are you almost ready? We're going to be late."

"Yes. I'll be out in a second."

I grab the cell phone and realize I've lost track of time. Jasen texted me forty-five minutes ago to let me know he was home and would get ready in the guest bedroom so he wouldn't rush me out of our master bathroom. I did it again. I just said *our* master bedroom.

I stand and grab the dress that's hanging in the bathroom closet. I slide out of the white silk robe I'm wearing and step into it. I decide not to wear any panties since the material is so thin. I slide the spaghetti straps over my shoulders. It fits perfectly, but I'm not surprised. Monroe and I wear the same size. The material is soft against my skin and hugs my curves. I reach for the platinum stilettos, put them on, and quickly clasp the straps together. I wobble a little as I find my balance. I'm sure I'll trip a few times before I get it together, but these heels are worth wearing tonight. I think about my conversation with my sister. Dressing sexy makes you feel sexy. And right now, I feel so sexy in this dress. I hope Jasen thinks so too. I open the bathroom door. His back is facing me. He has his cell phone glued to his ear, and when he turns around, his mouth drops open. He ends the call without a word and sweeps his eyes from the top of my head to the soles of my feet.

"Do you like it?" I ask.

He's wearing a black suit and looks yummy enough to eat. He tosses his cell phone on the nightstand and strides towards me. "You're stunning."

I blush. "You don't look so bad yourself. Let me just grab my clutch and we can go."

I step to his side and attempt to walk away, but he grasps my arm gently. "You don't need it."

"But it accents the dress," I explain.

"We're not leaving yet."

I wait for him to elaborate, and then it hits me. His eyes say it all. We're not leaving yet because he has plans for me. Plans that involve his body on top of mine, or under it, or behind it. However it happens, I'm eager to agree with whatever he has in store for me.

"Won't we miss our reservation? We're already running late," I ask in almost a whisper.

He pulls me to him closely. His left arm wraps around my waist tightly, and his right finger trails my cheek. Screw the restaurant and screw this date. I just want him. I need him. Nothing else matters at this moment besides quenching this thirst I have for him.

"Dinner can wait. Right now, I have other things in mind."

"Like?" I ask.

"Getting you out of this dress."

CHAPTER 10

JASEN

Once I saw her in that dress, I knew right then we wouldn't make it out of the house. We wouldn't make it past the doorway without me stripping her bare. My eyes rake her body. The dress she's wearing must be new because I don't recall seeing her wearing it before. Then again, Monroe has a wardrobe the size of Saks Fifth Avenue. The dress dips low, showcasing her cleavage. The spaghetti straps look thin enough to rip off, and there's no way she's wearing any panties with the way the material clings to her. My throat goes dry. Suddenly, my tie feels too tight, and the front of my pants feels strained.

She doesn't respond to my statement. Instead, she stares at me with eager eyes. I pull her in for a kiss, not caring about her strawberry-scented lipstick. My palms grip her ass, and I lift her up. She wraps her legs around me. I walk while carrying her. Once we reach the bed, I place her down on her feet. I step back and loosen my tie. "I need you out of that dress, Monroe."

Her breath hitches. She looks reluctant at first, but then her expression changes to anticipation. She slowly slips out of the dress. I'm already out of my shirt and tie. When she takes it off, I freeze with my hand on my zipper. Fuck me! She's not wearing any panties, just as I suspected. "You are the sexist woman walking this earth. I could come alone just by staring at you. Get on your knees, but keep the heels on."

She climbs on the bed and positions herself on her knees. I wasn't lying about what I said to her. I'm so hard it hurts. I unzip my pants and step out of them. Once I slide my boxer briefs down and step out of those, I join her on the bed. I place my hand at her upper shoulder, pushing her down slightly. "Arch your back for me."

She struggles at first. I don't know why. She's been in this position thousands of times. Maybe she's trying not to mess up her hair and makeup. I smirk when she's in the position I want her in. "You know what this position does to me. I want you to take all of me, okay?"

"Yes," she answers softly.

There's no time for foreplay right now. She ruined that the minute she stepped out of the bathroom in that dress. Right now, I just need to bury myself inside of her. My left hand caresses her lower back while my right hand finds her entrance. She's already wet, making it that much harder to contain myself. "You're already wet for me."

I waste no time easing into her. She tightens around me as I go deeper. I lean down and kiss her back. Then I move my fingers to her front, working her clit. She moans. She becomes wetter. Slippery. Allowing me to bury myself deep. My strokes start off slow, but she arches her back deeper, inviting me to pick up the pace. "Jasen, I..."

I know she's close. I can feel it. And it's only been a minute or so. But who's counting? When the chemistry is as hot as what we have, there's no time limit on pleasure. I squeeze her ass as I move in and out of her. I'm growing harder and harder by the second. "Fuck, you feel good."

She cries out as she tightens around me. "That's right, baby."

My body shudders as my own orgasm rocks me to my core. Her knees give out, and she falls flat, involuntarily pushing me out of her. I collapse beside her and trail my finger over her collarbone. "That was—"

"I know," I finish for her.

I remove a piece of hair that sticks to her face. The strand was once straight, but now it's frizzy from her sweat. "Sorry. I ruined your hair."

She smiles. "It's nothing that can't be fixed. Are we going to miss our reservation?"

"Do you care if we do?"

She exhales deeply. "No."

"Good. Because we're not leaving this bed."

We didn't make our reservation last night. But neither of us cared. We spent the night doing exactly what we needed to do— rediscovering our passion. We fell asleep in each other's arms until I snuck out early this morning for a run. My run went so well, I lost track of time. Monroe didn't seem to like the smoothie I bought for her last time, so I decide to pick her up a pastry instead. I feel on top of the world. I finally feel like my marriage is back on track, and it feels so fucking good. I never stopped loving her. Even during the tough times. But lately, seeing how much effort she's putting into our marriage, and me, makes me love her even more. The bell sounds as I enter the pastry shop. I'm not big on sweets, but the smell is so divine, I consider buying a pastry for myself as well. I lean down and peer inside the glass case, looking for something light and topped with fruit.

"Jasen?"

I stand tall and come face-to-face with Cooper's wife, Simone. "Hey, Simone."

"Picking up dessert?"

"Just finished my run and decided to pick up something for Monroe. She loves these things."

"How nice." Her tone suddenly shifts, indicating she didn't really mean what she said.

"How are you two doing anyway?"

"We've never been better."

There's a moment of silence. "Are you sure about that?"

I narrow my eyes. "Why do you ask?"

She shakes her head and smiles. "I'm sorry. I didn't mean to overstep. It's just, well... I just wanted to make sure you two were doing okay. I haven't seen you guys in a while."

"Yeah, it has been a long time. How about you? Are you feeling better?"

"What?"

"Cooper said you weren't feeling well."

"Did he now?"

"Yeah. He said he hated to leave without you."

"So he says."

"Excuse me?"

This conversation has turned awkward, and I don't know why. What I do know is that I'm getting the hell away from Simone and whatever it is that has her riled up this morning. "Well, I'd better be going. Monroe will wonder where I am."

I walk away when she calls after me. "You didn't buy your pastry."

I wave her off. "It's okay. I don't need it."

Monroe is awake when I arrive home. "Hey."

She hops off her stool and wraps her arms around my neck.

She kisses me gently. She's wearing one of my white T-shirts, and her hair is messy. She's looking sexy as hell this morning. So sexy, I want to lift her up and fuck her against the kitchen wall. But I don't. I'm sweating from my run, and the conversation with Simone has me unsettled. She unwraps her arms from around me and has a seat back at the counter. "I chopped some fresh fruit. And I had Otis bring in some fresh granola for you."

I walk over to the counter and grab the glass of orange juice she's poured for me. I drink the entire thing. I place the glass down and turn to face her. "I ran into Simone this morning."

She stops chewing. "She was acting really weird," I continue.

She chews the rest of her food. "Weird how?"

"She asked how we were doing. When I said we were doing well, she asked me was I sure."

"That is weird."

"Have you spoken to her? Did you tell her about our marital problems?"

"No. Not at all."

"Hmmm."

"What about Cooper? Have you told him about the problems we were having?"

I completely forgot about the conversation I had with Cooper. That's how she knows. That bastard broke bro-code 101. "I may have mentioned it to him."

She shrugs. "Well, there you go."

I grab a bowl of fruit and join her. "Yeah, it all makes sense now."

My phone rings. It's Cooper. "Monroe and I just spoke you up."

He's quiet for a second before he chuckles. "Is that so?"

"Yeah, I just ran into your wife at the pastry shop. She seemed *very* concerned about how Monroe and I were doing."

He laughs it off. "Simone is just nosey. Don't let it get to you.

Listen, do you remember that Josephs account I landed before I went out of town?"

"Yeah, the casino owner in Vegas."

"He's requesting I come meet him."

"For what?"

"He's into some heavy shit with the mob, and he's paranoid as shit. He doesn't trust me. He wants to speak in person. No phone. No email. Nothing."

"Cooper, I'm already up to my elbows juggling everything alone."

"I know. But this is important, Jasen. It's a huge account."

"How huge?"

"Five million dollars to find the mole in his company."

"Shit, that is huge. When will you be back?"

"I'll be back in a few days. I swear."

I take a deep breath. "Okay. I'll go. But I need you back. With you gone and Ariel fired, I—"

He interrupts me. "You fired Ariel?"

"Yeah."

"What the fuck for?"

I glance over at Monroe. "Long story."

I end the call and take a minute to think.

"What was that all about?"

"Cooper has an important client he needs me to meet with."

"Oh. Is he staying out of town longer than expected?"

"He said he'll be back in a few days, but apparently, this can't wait until then." I grab her hand. "Come with me to Vegas."

"I, ahh… I… I can't."

"Why not?"

"I don't want to be a distraction."

"You're never a distraction."

"Who will handle the office while you're gone? Maybe I should stay here and monitor the office until you get back."

"Sweetheart, is there a reason why you're making excuses not to join me?"

She swallows slowly, then shakes her head.

"The office will be fine. We'll stop by there on the way to the airport and forward the calls to my cell. I'll also put an out of office on saying to email me regarding urgent matters. Monroe. Come with me."

For some reason, she's hesitant. I thought she would be excited to come with me. She loves Vegas. She said that Vegas is exciting. Spunky. Just like her personality. Finally, her mouth curves in a smile. "Okay. I'll come."

MORGAN

I pace back and forth in the hotel room dialing Monroe again and again. I've been calling her since this morning, and she hasn't answered. I know I've hidden a lot from her, but this isn't something I can hide. I have to tell her about this trip. I know it'll upset her. But it's her fault I'm here. It's her fault Jasen thinks I'm her. Time and time again, I've asked her to dump Cooper and return home. Time and time again, I've told her she's making a huge mistake. But she won't listen. This is all her fault. Or is it? I guess I should own up to my responsibility in this. The plan was to act like her. I was supposed to be distant. Selfish. Uncaring. But I did the opposite. I've been treating Jasen like he's mine. Like we're two people in love. I've grown attached to him. I've grown to care about him. And not in the brother-in-law sense. The phone rings, startling me out of my thoughts. It's her.

"Hey."

"Hey, I'm sorry I missed your calls. Is everything okay? You've been calling me all morning."

"I know. Why didn't you answer?"

"Cooper and I ran out for lunch, and I accidently left the phone at the condo."

I take a deep breath before breaking the news. "Jasen asked me to come to Vegas with him for work."

"That's nothing unusual, Mo. He always asks me to come. He likes to turn them into romantic getaways. Just say you have plans."

"I… I tried."

"Tried? Wait, you went with him?"

"Yeah, I tried to make every excuse possible, but he was starting to wonder why I was reluctant to come."

"Let me get this straight. You're in Vegas, for a romantic getaway, with *my* husband?"

I'm instantly angered. "I didn't ask for this, Monroe."

"And I didn't ask for you to go outside the script either. What's next? Are you going to fuck him too?"

I don't answer her. "Oh my God. Tell me you didn't."

Jasen walks in, interrupting my call. "I gotta go."

"Morgan, don't you—" I end the call before I can answer her question.

Tears sting my eyes, but I can't let them fall. Jasen will wonder what's wrong. "Hey, are you okay?"

He watches me with concern, but I don't give in. I can't give in. "Yeah, I'm just a little tired."

I'm hurting right now. I'm hurting because I've betrayed my sister. I'm hurting because Jasen is too good for me to be deceiving him like I have. I'm also angry. Angry at Monroe for asking me to do this, and angry at myself for agreeing. "Understood. Here, I went to the gift shop and bought you a charger since you forgot yours."

"Thank you."

"I've got to make a call in an hour or so, but we can hang out after that if you want."

"I can't wait. I've never been to Vegas before."

I walk past him and plug the charger into the USB port. I have over ten missed calls from Monroe already, so I place the phone on silent and attach it to the charger. I spin around to find Jasen staring at me. "What's wrong?"

"You just said you've never been to Vegas before."

"I haven't."

"I thought you were here for a bachelorette party. Remember your friend from the massage parlor got married?"

My stomach drops. Why didn't Monroe tell me this just now. Probably because she figured out I slept with Jasen. "Oh yeah. I mean, we were confined to the room most of the time."

He cocks his head to the side. "You sent me videos of you guys in the strip club. And you almost maxed out my card at the restaurants and casinos."

Fuck!

I wave him off. "You know what? You're right. I was so drunk I don't even remember."

He stares at me for a few seconds, but his cell phone rings, distracting him. He looks at the caller. "I've gotta take this."

Jasen left for his client meeting, and I took the time to take a nap. Not only was I exhausted from the short flight, but I was also mentally exhausted from my earlier conversation from Monroe. I ignored all twenty-three calls and thirteen text messages. I figured it would be best to let her calm down before we speak again. I slept peacefully until Jasen returned a few hours later and climbed into bed with me. He made love to me, twice. I dozed off again with him lying beside me this time. I'm wakened when his cell phone rings. He groans before rolling over to answer it. "Yeah."

He's quiet for a second. "It went well. We got the account. Yup, I'm still here. The wife and I are going to explore before we head home. Yeah, yeah, just hurry back. I'm drowning here."

He ends the call. "Who was that?" I know the answer, but I need him to confirm it.

He rolls over to face me. "Cooper."

Just as I thought. I wonder if Monroe put Cooper up to calling Jasen because I haven't returned her calls. Is she checking up on me? "What did he want?"

"To see how the meeting went, which he could've asked in a text."

She is definitely checking up on me.

"Don't worry about him. He won't be bothering us again."

He leans in and kisses my neck. His hand slips under the blanket. But I'm not in the mood. I stop his hand from reaching my inner thigh. "I'm still sore."

It's not a complete lie. I am still sore from earlier. Jasen is well-endowed. But I'm mentally distracted. All I can think about is what Monroe must be thinking, which is the worst. And she'd be right. "Are you sure you're okay?"

I nod. "I'm okay."

He searches my eyes for something, but what, I don't know. He moves a piece of hair away from my face. "I don't think you have any idea how much I love you."

I don't. And I don't think Monroe does either.

I almost cry. I almost tell him the truth. He's in love with his wife. A wife who couldn't care less about his feelings. A wife who has made it clear she's in love with someone else. He shouldn't love her. Because she doesn't love him. But it's hard to tell him this. Because although Monroe doesn't love him... I do.

MONROE

I'm fucking livid with Morgan. Going to Vegas with Jasen? That was not part of the plan. She took it upon herself to make that decision without consulting me first. She knows I wouldn't have agreed. I barely traveled with Jasen. But that's not the reason I'm pissed. I'm pissed because I'm starting to think that Morgan is forgetting this isn't real. She's forgetting that Jasen is my husband, not hers. Time and time again, she's told me I'm making a mistake. That I need to end things with Cooper and work things out with my husband. And I refused. But now I'm thinking she's right. I've made a huge mistake. Cooper said that Jasen has sounded happy lately. Happier than he's been in a long time. And it's because Morgan hasn't done a damn thing we agreed on. I knew she couldn't act like me. No matter how much I tried to teach her. If she had stuck with the plan, Jasen would still be miserable. This way, it would be much easier to ask for a divorce when Cooper and I return. I'm hit with a feeling I didn't think was possible: jealousy. The thought of Jasen being happy with someone else makes me green with envy. And the thought of him sleeping with my own sister makes me furious. I asked her if she'd slept with him. She didn't answer. I've been calling her constantly, but no response. I'm going crazy wondering what is going on between them. I need answers. And I need them now.

I guess I've always known it would come to this at some point or another. I love Jasen, but I don't think I ever really fell in love with him. I love him dearly, and I really tried to be the best wife that I could be. But I don't love him the way he loves me. I don't know what's wrong with me. Jasen is a good man. Most women would think they hit the jackpot. But not me. I've been unhappy for a long time. And who's to say it won't happen with Cooper? I'm a free spirit. Sexually fluid. Is it possible for me to settle down with any man?

"There you are," Cooper says as he steps onto the balcony.

"Hey."

The sunrays bounce off his skin as he steps forward. "You've been out here for hours."

"I needed time to think."

He takes a seat beside me. "Are you okay?"

My eyes meet his, and my heart melts. I really care for Cooper. But some small piece of me knows it won't be long before I get bored with him also. I'm not capable of love. I know because although I love both Jasen and Cooper, my love is conditional. Fleeting. What's the use of leaving my husband for a man who I'll most likely get tired of at some point? I should get rid of them both and live single and free. "Do you think we're doing the right thing?"

He grabs my hand. "Yes. We love each other, right?"

I nod. "But is that enough?"

He cocks his head to the side. "Are you having second thoughts?"

"No, I..."

"What is it?"

"I'm just not sure this is right, Cooper. Are we only happy with each other because we're unhappy with our spouses?"

He jerks his hand away. "Are you really asking me that? Monroe, I'm willing to risk everything for you. Do you think Jasen and I will still be partners once he finds out? Do you think Simone will let this go easily? Jesus, she's going to try to take me for everything I've got. But I don't care about any of that. I don't care because I love you."

I shut my eyes tightly. I knew what the risks were. But hearing him name them makes me feel guilty. "Cooper, I love you too. I'm just saying that maybe we should take a step back and *really* think about what we're doing."

He pushes to his feet angrily. "I know exactly what I'm doing. I knew what I was doing the minute I fucked you. All those hours spent in hotel rooms. All the late-night phone calls. I knew what I was getting into. I knew what I wanted. And I thought you felt the same."

I rise to my feet slowly. "You know how I feel about you, Cooper."

"No. I thought I knew. Right now, I have no idea what's going on with you."

I place my hands on my hips. "I don't like your tone."

He huffs. "And I don't like the fact that the woman I'm in love with thinks she can just turn this on and off like a fucking faucet. Listen to me and listen good, Monroe. We're in this deep now. And I'm not letting you go."

"What the hell does that mean?" I ask.

He watches me with piercing eyes. "It means we've fallen in love with each other. And even though it may be wrong that it happened, we've made our bed. Now we're going to lie in it... together."

CHAPTER 11

MORGAN

I lie awake and stare at the ceiling, wondering if I'm about to do the right thing. I tossed and turned all night, riddled with guilt and shame about what I've been doing. I can't do this anymore. I'm done lying. I'm done pretending. I've got to come clean with Jasen, even if it means throwing my sister under the bus. I didn't think I would fall for him. Especially this quickly. But I did. He enters the hotel room carrying his briefcase. "Hey."

I rise and sit at the edge of the bed. "Hey."

He places his briefcase on the table. "I figured we could..."

He stops speaking as he walks towards me. "Hey, are you okay?"

I'm not okay. I've been crying, and I'm sure my swollen, red eyes give it away. "Sweetheart, what's wrong?"

I open my mouth to tell him, but nothing comes out. This is harder than I thought it would be. He's going to hate Monroe for what she's done. He's going to hate the both of us. "I..."

I choke as the tears fall harder and the sobs rock me gently.

He falls to his knees and wraps his arms around my waist. "Baby, tell me, what is it?"

"I'm sorry. I'm so sorry."

It's all I can muster. All I can do right now is apologize for something he has no idea has happened. He wipes my tears away with his thumb. "It's okay. Whatever it is, it's okay."

You don't understand. It's not okay.

I sniffle. He stands to his feet, grabs some tissues, and hands them to me. I take them and blow my nose. When my nose is clear and my tears have lessened, I look up at him. "I'm sorry. You deserve so much better."

He shakes his head, then drops back to his knees. He reaches in his pocket and pulls out a little black box. When he opens it, my heart stops beating. "I have everything I want and need right here in front of me. I know we've had our issues, but I've never stopped loving you. I want to renew our vows, Monroe. Will you marry me... again?"

My eyes are so big I feel like they'll pop out of my head. It's become worse than I thought. Jasen is on his knees asking who he thinks is his wife to marry him. I have two choices here. I can decline and tell him everything. Stop this from going any further. Or I can say yes and fall deeper into this web of deception.

JASEN

She hasn't answered me. And I'm afraid she'll say no. Monroe didn't get a proper proposal last time. We were lying in bed after making love when I said, "Let's get married."

But with everything going so smoothly lately, I wanted to do a do-over proposal. I got up early this morning and went to the nearest jewelry store. I bought her the best upgrade I could find. The diamond is huge. Something she can wear with pride and flash every chance she gets. Her original ring is nice, but it's simple. Plain. I didn't have much money when I purchased it. And as things spiraled with us over the years, she stopped wearing it. And I stopped caring. But now... Now I want a fresh start. Starting with a new ring. I was going to wait until dinner tonight to propose, but seeing her this vulnerable, apologizing for everything she's done, made me drop to one knee right then and there. I couldn't let her beat herself up about the way she acted. I wanted her to know that it's all in the past. I search her eyes. "Baby, say something."

She stares at the ring with wide, teary eyes. Her lips are slightly parted. Finally, she answers. "Yes."

I take her left hand and slide the ring on. It's tighter than it should be, but it goes on after some force. Once it's sitting perfectly on her finger, I kiss her. I pull away when I feel her body heat through the hotel robe she's wearing. "Do you like it?"

"It's beautiful."

"We're going to do it right this time. A small intimate wedding with close family and friends."

I don't have a lot of friends. I've always been a loner and still am. I hardly ever hang out, besides the occasional beer with Cooper. Monroe is the same. She doesn't have many friends. But she does have acquaintances. Women she's met at the salon or at the nail place she frequents. They get together and shop. They have spa dates while sipping champagne and talking about absolutely nothing. I know because she hosted a pool party at the house one day. I was curious to know who these women were, so I eavesdropped. The conversation revolved around the latest designs. Hollywood's elite. And how much their husbands spoil them. By the end of the conversation, I was convinced she was using them for companionship. Monroe has never been as close to anyone as she was with her sister. And when they had a falling-out, I think she felt lonely. But her pride wouldn't allow her to make things right. The timing of them making up is perfect. When we got married the first time, Morgan didn't make it to our ceremony at the courthouse. I never knew why. But now, she can have her sister here. "Morgan can come this time. Why don't you invite her to the house for the weekend? Spend some time with her and wedding plan. I'm sure you'd rather plan with her than those other women you hang around."

"Yeah, yeah, I'd like that a lot."

MORGAN

After we showered and dressed, Jasen and I decided to have dinner.

"Have you been to Top of the World at the Stratosphere Hotel?"

"No."

"Good. That's where we're going. The food is great, and it's romantic."

"Okay."

The Uber arrives just as his cell phone rings. He answers it once we've settled inside. "Yeah."

He's quiet for a minute. "Are you telling me it's *he* who's been doing the cheating? Well, this changes everything."

More silence. "Okay. Send me what you got. Thanks, Roberto."

He ends the call. "Who's Roberto?"

"He's one of our spies."

I gasp. "You have spies?"

He faces me with a look of surprise. "Monroe, you knew this already. And before you ask, the answer is no. I cannot tell you about this case. You know my clients are confidential."

"Yup, got it."

The Uber pulls in front of the Stratosphere, and Jasen grabs my hand. We exit the car and head inside. Once we exit the elevator, we're met by the hostess. "May I help you?"

"Reservation for Mr. and Mrs. Baker."

Baker isn't my last name, but I love the sound of it. "Right this way."

She leads us to our table, and it takes my breath away. We're so high up we can see the entire city. One side of it anyway. I'm able to get a full view as we spin around slowly. I can barely feel it. "This is beautiful."

He grabs my hand. "A beautiful view for my beautiful wife."

I squeal excitedly as Jasen shuts the door behind us. "I can't believe I won three grand."

It's a little after three in the morning, but I'm still feeling the high. After our romantic dinner, Jasen and I casino hopped. We drank. We gambled. We laughed. I had a blast. As a matter of fact, this is the most fun I've ever had in my entire life. I drink moderately. I don't gamble. And I'm usually in bed by ten most nights. I've never let loose like this. I've never just let my hair down to be completely free. I was always concerned about my morals or worrying about what others would think. Well, screw the morals. Who cares what anyone thinks? I'm a grown-ass woman who can do what she wants. I've wasted too many years being Boring Betty. I've missed out on so much fun trying to be the good twin. Fuck it! It's time I start living. This is the new me now. And no, it's not the alcohol that's talking. Okay, maybe the alcohol is talking a little bit.

"I can't believe it either. Especially after you lost a thousand dollars the first time."

My face scrunches with a look of horror. "I lost a thousand dollars?"

He chuckles. "Yup."

I plop down on the bed. "Oh my gosh. I'm so… sorry, Jasen."

I'm slurring my words, but I'm sure he gets the point.

The bed dips as he sits beside me. "Hey, we had a good time. I don't care about the money."

I turn on my side to face him. "This was the best night of my life. Thank you."

I suddenly feel emotional because I know this will all end soon. Jasen has shown me that true love does exist. He's shown me another side of me. I was able to show him all of me, and he loved me anyway. It's funny, Monroe and I are like night and day, yet he seems to love how he *thinks* she's changed. He loves the new her. Only the new her is really me. Maybe Monroe was right—maybe they aren't compatible. I shake away the thought that comes next. Maybe it's me he's more compatible with.

Stop it! You know that'll never happen.

"There's more where this came from, baby. We're going to date more often, I promise."

His phone vibrates with a text. His expression grows grim as he reads it. "What is it?"

"We have to cut our trip short. I've got some business at home I need to handle. I'm sorry, baby."

"It's okay. What time are we leaving?"

He climbs on top of me. "As soon as I'm done making love to you."

MORGAN

The sunlight beams brightly through the window, causing my eyes to pop open. I turn over, reaching for Jasen, but he's gone. A note rests in his spot. I grab the note and read it. I Love You!

I smile as I stretch my arms and rise from the bed. I'm not sure what time we arrived in Los Angeles, but I crashed as soon as we got here. I remember Jasen carrying me upstairs and placing me in bed. I blush as I think about the naughty things he did to me in Vegas. I can still feel the ache between my legs. I came to the decision that I'm going to tell Monroe. Everything.

And once she knows the truth about what I've done, I'll tell Jasen. The phone vibrates with an incoming text.

Monroe: Call me. It's important.

I call her immediately. She answers on the first ring. "Is there any reason why you ignored my calls? My messages?"

"I'm sorry. I couldn't talk with Jasen around."

The line grows silent, and I immediately know something is wrong. And not because Monroe is hardly ever quiet, but because our twin empathy does work sometimes. And right now, I can feel something is off. "Something's wrong."

"I need to talk to you. Can you come here?"

"With Cooper there?"

"He's not here. I'll text you the address."

"Okay."

"Morgan. Please hurry."

When Monroe said that she and Cooper were on a getaway, I assumed they were way out of reach. Turns out, they were in Santa Monica. It took me over an hour to get there, due to traffic. I exit the car and am immediately smacked with the salty ocean breeze. The door swings open before I have the chance to knock. "Took you long enough," she snaps.

"I was in traffic."

I follow her inside and into the kitchen. There's an empty wine bottle on the table. "You drank the entire bottle?"

She grabs another bottle out of the refrigerator, pops the cork, and places it on the table. She grabs another wineglass and takes a seat. "I'm stressed the fuck out, Mo."

I sit across from her. "What happened?"

She pours the wine in both glasses and shoves one towards me. She takes a huge gulp before she answers me. "I think I made a mistake."

My body stiffens. My heart beats loudly. I wasn't expecting to hear those words. And although I should be happy, I'm not. "Did you hear me?"

"Yes."

"I can't be with Cooper."

"What... what's changed?"

The tears slide down her cheeks. "I've reached the conclusion that I'm not relationship material. I'll never be able to commit to anyone. It's only a matter of time before I get tired of Cooper. Just like I got tired of Jasen."

"I don't understand."

"Morgan, think about it. I've always been a free spirit. I've never liked rules. Structure. Predictability."

"Have you told him?"

"Yeah. He got all pissed off. He started throwing shit and accusing me of leading him on. And he's right, Mo. I made him think we had a future together. That leaving our spouses was for the best."

She cries softly, and I'm floored. I haven't seen Monroe cry since she accidently got shampoo in her eyes when we were kids. She didn't even cry at Grandma Rose's funeral. I move to comfort her. "It's going to be okay."

She shakes her head. "No. It's not. What is wrong with me, Mo? Why can't I be like normal women?"

"Because you're *you*, Monroe. And that's okay. What do *you* want? What will make you happy."

She sniffles. "I just want to live, Morgan. No husband. No kids. No structure. I want to get up in the morning and fly to New York just because. I want to sleep with whomever I want to sleep with, with no strings attached. I want to go on adventures with different people. I want freedom. That's the life I've always wanted."

I finally ask the question that's been burning in my brain. "Are you still planning to divorce Jasen?"

"Yes."

I nod.

She leans back in her chair, wineglass in hand. "You fucked him, didn't you?"

"I…"

"That wasn't part of the plan. How could you do something so treacherous, sleeping with your sister's husband?"

I see red. "Oh no. Don't make me out to be the bad guy here. Did you forget I liked him first?"

She huffs. "Is that what made you do it? Because you had some silly-ass crush on him in high school? Face it, Morgan, *he* chose *me*."

"And are you sure that would've been the case had he known that I liked him? What makes you think that you were the better twin for him?"

"He married me, didn't he?"

"Yeah, and look where that's gonna get him. This is going to crush him when he finds out."

She stands up. "What he if he never finds out?"

"What do you mean?"

"I need to get away. What if we never tell the truth? We can just switch lives."

"You mean you want me to pretend to be you permanently?"

"Don't sound so offended, Mo. I'm sure you're enjoying yourself. After all, you did fuck him."

I don't respond, and she watches me carefully. "You have feelings for him."

I can't deny it anymore. All this lying is tearing me apart. "Yes."

She rolls her eyes and laughs spitefully. "I guess that's what I get for putting you in this situation."

"The more I tried to be you, the harder it became. I became myself, but a better version, and I started to care about him."

"So, you see why we need to do this?"

"Monroe. I just told you I care about Jasen. If we do this…"

"I know. I know exactly what will happen if we do this."

We stare at each other as her unspoken words pass to me. Her eyes say that she knows I'll fall in love with him.

I shake my head. "If we do this, there's no turning back. I'm not going to lie for the next fifteen years and make it much worse now that he thinks he's fallen in love all over again."

She shakes her head in return. "We won't turn back."

I take a deep breath. "So, what do we do now?"

"We move forward with our next plan. You get Jasen out of the house tomorrow, and I'll come home and pack. I've got so much shit he'll never realize some of it's missing."

"Okay. I'll text him when I leave here and tell him I want to spend the day with him."

"Good. That gives me plenty of time to pack."

"Then where will you go?"

"I don't know yet, sis." She smiles. "All I know is that I'll finally be free."

"What about Cooper?"

"Easy fix. I'll meet with him before I leave and break things off."

A tear slides down my cheek at the idea of Monroe running off to God knows where. She must feel my pain because she starts to cry as well. "Will I see you soon?"

She shakes her head. "Not at first. Give me time to adjust to my new life, then we can see each other."

"Okay."

"I'm sorry I dragged you into this, sis, but look at the bright side—you finally got your guy."

Sadness crosses her face, and I grab her hand. "That's not more important than my relationship with you."

She smiles. "I love you, Morgan, and we'll be closer than ever after this."

I smile back. "I love you too, Monroe."

CHAPTER 12

MORGAN

"Just a few more steps."

The bandana sits snug against my eyes, preventing me from seeing. Jasen guides my arm gently as my sandals hit the ground beneath me carefully. I allow him to guide me with each anticipating step. "Are we there yet?"

He chuckles from behind me. "Almost."

We're outside, and the weather is perfect. I'm wearing a crimson sundress with crème sandals. I can feel the slight breeze blowing my loose curls. It's quiet apart from the sounds of the birds chirping. "Right here."

We stop, but he doesn't remove the bandana yet. I extend my arms in front of me, thinking I might feel something. But I don't. "The suspense is killing me."

He lets go of my arm and unties the bandana. My eyes blink rapidly to adjust. But when the image before me becomes clearer, I gasp. "A picnic!" A huge white blanket is spread underneath a tree, decorated with fresh red rose petals. A basket sits atop the blanket, along with a bucket of ice with champagne. "Jasen, this is beautiful."

He guides me down, and when I'm seated, he joins me. He removes the champagne and pops the cork. "When you suggested I take the day off, I knew I wanted to do something romantic with you." He pours us both a glass and hands me mine. "And I'm enjoying dating you. That's something we didn't do much."

He's piqued my interest.

"You don't feel like we got to date?"

He takes a minute to think. "No. I couldn't afford it in high school. I couldn't afford it when we first moved here. And by the time I became wealthy, we were past the honeymoon phase. Besides the occasional dinner, we don't do anything romantic. Now that we're getting back on track, I'm taking the opportunity to court you."

"Oh."

"I like where we are. Things are going to be different now."

"How so?"

He takes a sip of his champagne, and I follow suit. When he's finished swallowing, he answers my question. "It was never about the money with you, Monroe. I like that I can provide for my wife. I like buying you nice things. But I felt that was all it was. A Hermès bag could light up your face like a dozen roses couldn't. But now that you're changing... I mean, now that *we're* changing, I want to do nice things for you that don't require money. Show you how special you are to me."

My smile couldn't be wider. "Money is good, but romance is better."

He laughs. "We weren't saying that when we could barely keep the lights on back then."

I chuckle. "No. I guess we weren't."

"I'm grateful, and I feel incredibly lucky to be blessed with a great career and an amazing wife."

"Speaking of career. Who's running the office with you being out today?"

"Cooper. He has something personal to take care of this afternoon, and then he's going to head to the office to catch up on some things."

My heart skips a beat. Monroe must have already called him to meet with her this afternoon. He places his glass down and opens the basket. He pulls out a plate of fresh strawberries and places one against my lips. I take a bite and smile with satisfaction at the burst of flavor. Today is perfect. This date is perfect. Jasen... is perfect.

"Are you excited about the wedding?"

I'm about to answer him when my phone rings. It's Monroe. "Hey."

His phone rings right after mine, and he stands to answer it.

"I just called to tell you I'm at the house. I've already called Cooper, and he's going to meet me in an hour. After that, I'm heading south."

"Okay, sounds good."

Jasen walks away as he chats on the phone.

"Do you need anything?"

"No. I have everything I need."

"Money?"

"No. I have a stash of cash hidden that Jasen never knew about."

"Oh."

"Remember what Grandma Rose taught us?"

"Never let your right hand know what your left hand is doing?" We say it in unison, laughing afterwards.

"I was smart enough to stash money that Jasen would give me for shopping. But if I happen to run out, there's a diamond bracelet in my jewelry box. Jasen gave it to me for our anniversary, and it's worth over fifty grand. Could you put it up someplace safe for me? Just in case I need you to sell it and send me the money?

"Of course."

"Thank you. Well, I guess this is it."

"I guess it is."

"I'll call you when I'm safe somewhere."

"Okay."

I end the call just as Jasen takes a seat beside me. "Sorry, that was Cooper. He had a question about a meeting scheduled for tomorrow."

"It's okay."

"Who were you talking to?"

"My sister."

"Everything alright between you two?"

"Yup. Everything is just fine."

"Good. Are you ready to eat?"

"Sure. What did you make?"

"Ham and cheese."

"Ugh, I hate ham."

He pauses. "What are you talking about? Ham and cheese is one of your favorites."

It's one of Monroe's favorites. Mine is turkey and cheese. I despise ham, but I didn't mean to let it slip.

"I mean, I do love ham. I just haven't had any good ham lately. I've been eating turkey instead."

He removes the sandwiches from the basket. "Oh, well, then you can have mine."

He hands me the sandwich, and when I go to grab it, he pulls it back and grabs my hand. He brings it to his lips. "I'm going to make you the happiest woman in the world."

I smile with eyes full of tears. "I already am."

A few hours later, we decide to head home. The picnic was a success. Jasen explained that he wasn't sure I'd like it at first considering I hate the outdoors. I laugh to myself at the thought of Monroe sitting outside under a tree. He's spot-on. She would have hated every second of it. Me, on the other hand, I loved it. I was happy that he took the time to plan a romantic date for us. He's just started the car, and we're on our way home. His cell phone rings, and he stares at the number before answering it. I watch his expression turn grim as he listens to the person on the other end. His eyes bulge from their sockets, and his expression turns to pure terror. I immediately grab his hand. "What's wrong?" I whisper.

"Yes, we'll be right there."

He ends the call. "What is it?"

He looks straight ahead and speaks with devastation. "Your sister. She was at our house, and something's happened to her."

JASEN

We arrive at the house, and it's like a scene from *Law and Order*. Police are swarming the area, and there's yellow tape everywhere. We step out of the car and rush to the front door. A policewoman stops us. "I'm sorry, but I can't let you in."

"This is my house," I say sternly.

She nods. "I understand. But I have strict instructions not to let anyone in."

I'm about to argue further when a detective approaches us. "Are you Mr. and Mrs. Baker?"

"Yes, we are."

He places his hand on her shoulder. "They're okay."

She steps to the side and allows us to pass through. We follow him inside. It's total chaos. "What's happened?" Monroe asks frantically.

The detective stops when we reach the living room. "I'm Detective Henby."

He's tall. About six feet, with light brown eyes and a serious demeanor. "Can you tell us where the two of you were around 3:00 p.m.?"

"I took my wife on a date. We had a picnic at Griffith Park."

He writes down our answers as my wife moves closer beside me. "Please, tell us what's going on."

He takes a deep breath. Then his eyes focus on Monroe. "Ma'am, are you related to a Morgan Vaughn?"

"Yes, she's my twin sister."

He nods. "I figured as such. The resemblance is scary."

She reaches for my hand and squeezes tightly. "Where is she? Is she in some kind of trouble?"

He hesitates for a minute before he gives us the news. "She was murdered."

She collapses in my arms, soaking me with tears. "No."

I hold her tightly, trying my best to comfort her. "Where?"

"Upstairs, the hallway outside the master bedroom."

"When was the last time either of you spoke to her?" he continues.

"She called my wife this afternoon."

He writes something down. "Did you know she was going to be here? Her driver's license has a Philadelphia address."

Monroe nods. "She did mention something about flying out to surprise me. We were supposed to start wedding planning."

"And you didn't hear from her after that?"

"No."

"Looks like your housekeeper let her in. We interviewed her, and she indicated that she arrived around 3:00 p.m. Shortly after that, your business partner arrived."

"Cooper?"

He looks down at his notes. "Cooper Tilley?"

"What would he be doing here?'

"We don't know, but we're going to find out."

I'm dumbfounded. Cooper knew I wasn't home. I told him I

was out on a date with Monroe when he called me earlier. "What did Lula say?"

"She said she finished her shift right after. She thought you were aware of them both coming over."

"My wife explained that Morgan came here to surprise her. But Cooper? We have no idea why he would have come here. Especially knowing that I wouldn't be home. I told him earlier that Monroe and I were on a date."

He takes more notes. "We've been trying to locate him for questioning."

Monroe finally releases me and sniffles. "Have you checked with his wife?"

"Yes. She hasn't seen him since he left for work this morning."

Monroe nods. "Can I see my sister?"

He shakes his head. "I'm sorry, but it's procedure. You won't be able to see her until you identify the body."

She becomes tense, and I become agitated. I have questions. Questions I need answered. In addition, my wife is hurting, and there is nothing I can do right now to make it better for her. "Detective, is there anything else you can tell us about what happened here?"

The detective wants to oppose, but he doesn't. "I understand you both have concerns, but all I can tell you right now is that it's early in the investigation. As we gather more details, we'll let you know."

"This can't be happening," Monroe says softly.

Detective Henby takes a step forward. "I'm sorry."

Monroe buries her face in my chest. Detective Henby gives me a look of sympathy and allows her the time to release her uncontrollable cries. Once she settles down a little, he continues to speak. "We'll need for you to identify the body as soon as possible."

Monroe becomes uneasy, which is understandable. She just

lost her sister. Her *twin* sister. She's in no shape to do this tonight. "Can it wait until tomorrow? When she's a lot calmer."

He nods with understanding. "Sure. I understand. We'll wrap up here as soon as we're done collecting evidence."

I hold Monroe tighter. "Take your time. We'll book a hotel room for the night."

He reaches inside his pocket and pulls out a business card. He passes one to each of us. "You'll be hearing from me soon. But if either of you have any questions or remember anything, please give me call."

CHAPTER 13

MORGAN: TWO WEEKS LATER

I sit at the table of my Philadelphia home replaying everything in my head. In the past few weeks, I pretended to be my sister. Fell in love with her husband. And buried her. My sister is dead, and now I'm stuck between continuing the lie or coming clean once and for all. Jasen pulls out a chair beside me. "How are you holding up?"

"I can't believe she's gone."

He places his hand over top of mine. "We'll get through this, Monroe."

I close my eyes at the sound of my sister's name. My heart shatters at the realization that I'll never see her or speak to her again. I feel horrible. None of this was supposed to happen. I was being selfish by agreeing to switch lives for good. I should have done what was right. If I had, maybe she would still be alive.

"Detective Henby will be stopping by a little later, once the repass is over," he says to me cautiously.

"He's here? In Philly?"

"Yeah."

"Why?"

"It's not unusual for detectives to attend funerals for victims. They like to scout the crowd, see if they see anyone suspicious."

"Oh."

"Are you going to be okay to talk to him?"

I nod.

"Sweetheart, are you sure?"

"Yeah. I just... I want to get this over with."

"Okay." He kisses me on top of the head before he stands and exits the kitchen.

The process to bury Monroe was a grueling one. The detectives needed to keep her body in California until the official autopsy report was released. Once that was complete, her body was released to us. We then had to arrange to have it shipped to Philadelphia, and that's where the headache began. I had to get a burial transport permit and work closely with the airline to have it transported in a timely fashion. Everything was lined up. Until I got a call that the airline delivered her to the wrong state. Apparently, there's a *Henry Ella Funeral Home* in South Carolina as well. It was a nightmare. I spent hours on the phone with the airline as well as the funeral home. It cost me additional money to have it delivered back to the airport and placed on a plane to be delivered to the correct funeral home. By the time she got here, two weeks had passed, and I didn't want to have an open-casket funeral. She didn't look the same. That, and I couldn't bear to look at her that way. Identifying her body was bad enough.

I sat numb during her funeral today. I kept wondering if she would have been happy with the way things turned out. I concluded that she wouldn't. She's probably turning over in her fresh grave already. Her funeral was boring. Why? Because it's supposed to be me lying in that casket. And I'm the boring one.

She lay in a white casket, surrounded with flowers, while the choir from my grandmother's church sang slow and sad songs. Monroe would have wanted to be buried in a red casket because it was her favorite color. She would have wanted bamboo plants in place of flowers because those were her favorites. She would have wanted party music played so everyone could dance and have a good time. And she would have had more people in attendance. More than the few family and coworkers of mine who attended today. I hosted the repass here at the house we grew up in. The house I lived in before going to California. Jasen recommended I pack up her belongings so I don't have to worry about coming back here. So, I did.

We stayed at a hotel the night Monroe was murdered. That next morning, we went down to the station, where we were questioned further by Detective Henby. He explained that they were actively searching for Cooper, but he couldn't be found. To make matters worse, Simone was having a hard time coming to grips with what had happened. She had so many questions about why Cooper would come to our home and kill a woman he didn't know. It makes me anxious as well. When the detective asked about her being there, I had to quickly lie to Jasen and pretend that she flew out to surprise me. Thank goodness the housekeeper let her in, otherwise, I have no idea how I would have explained that. But Simone has a point. Cooper killing a woman he doesn't know doesn't add up. And I'm sure the detectives feel the same way. I know the truth. Monroe said she would meet with Cooper to break it off with him. My guess is that he wasn't happy about it and killed my sister. They have the evidence. His prints were found on the blade that killed her. But they're missing his motive. And they're missing him. If they find him, the truth could come out.

Jasen walks in. "People are starting to leave. Do you want to come say goodbye to them?"

"Sure, I'll be in in a second."

He nods and walks out of the room. I stand to smooth my black dress out and prepare to greet my family and friends… as Monroe.

I enter the living room, where friends and family stand around nibbling on hors d'oeuvres. No one suspects a thing. I work the room, hugging each person and thanking them for coming. It's weird hearing what people think of me. Each person says things like *Morgan was so responsible. She took such great care of Rose when she got sick. She was so smart. Such a hard worker. Such a great person. She had a good heart.* Boring. Boring. Boring. I suddenly see why Monroe tried her best to live every day to the fullest. Why she tried her best to enjoy her life as much as possible. She wanted to be happy, even if it meant she had to hurt someone in the process. I hug my aunt Peggy tightly. "Monroe, maybe you'll visit us more now."

I nod, promising that I will. It's a lie though. I don't plan on visiting her at all. I haven't seen her since I was a kid. People say the most cliché things at funerals. *Sorry for your loss. She's in a better place. I'm here for you.* And my favorite, *Let me know if you need anything.* Most don't mean any of it. They only say those things because they think it'll make you feel better, comforted to a certain extent, when in fact, all it does is irritate you. I've said my goodbyes to everyone and exhale loudly when I close the door behind the last person to leave. Jasen leads me to the living room "Won't you relax?"

I plop down in the leather recliner, my grandmother's favorite, and kick my heels off. He gets down on one knee and takes my right foot into his hands. He does a combination of stroking it and kneading it with pressure. The soreness eases as he rubs them firmly. I hadn't realized just how many hours I've been wearing my heels until now. A moan escapes me but is quickly interrupted when the doorbell rings. Jasen's hands stop. "It's probably the detective."

I groan loudly but not from pleasure. I don't want to do this right now. "It'll be fine, Monroe." He gently places my foot down and goes to open the door. He enters the living room a minute later with Detective Henby by his side.

"I won't keep you guys long."

"Any luck finding Cooper?" Jasen asks.

He shakes his head. "Cell towers place him at your house around the time the crime was committed but nowhere else after that."

"Has Simone heard from him yet?" I ask.

"She hasn't heard anything either. Poor thing is a wreck. To find out your husband murdered someone is just..." He pauses. "Horrible."

"Yes. It is," Jasen agrees.

"We have his fingerprints from a background check done by his previous employer. It's a 100 percent match. We just need to find him to gather the motive and charge him."

Jasen looks at me with tears in his eyes. "I'm sorry. I had no idea Cooper would..." He shakes his head. "I can't believe he would do something like this."

"How close were you and Cooper?" the detective asks.

"We were close regarding the business. But we didn't disclose much of our personal lives. He's very private, and so am I."

"So, you two never hung out outside of work?"

"We went out for a beer occasionally, and we had dinner together with our families twice."

He writes something down as Jasen continues to speak. "I've known him since high school. He's extremely smart. Straight A student. Valedictorian. And kept to himself. We ended up working together at a security firm and soon found out we didn't like it there. So, we went into business together. For as long as I've known him, he's been reliable. Sharp. I can't for the life of me understand why he would do something like this." His eyes swing over to mine. "This just doesn't make sense."

The detective turns to face me. "Although his fingerprints are a match, we still need to conduct a full investigation. That means interviewing friends and family. Ruling out other suspects. Did your sister have any enemies that you're aware of?"

"No. She barely had any friends."

It's the truth. Outside of Linda from work, I literally have no friends.

"There's no one you can think of who knew she was traveling to Los Angeles?"

"No," I reply.

He nods. "We've been trying to locate her cell phone. Trace her last steps. But we've been unable to find it. Looks like Cooper fled with it."

"Any way you can track it?" Jasen asks.

"We've tried. No luck."

I stand to my feet. "What's next?"

"We've interviewed your sister's coworkers, ran her background, and screened her social media accounts. Right now, all we can do is continue with the investigation until we get a lead."

He places his mini notebook back in his pocket. "We'll let you know if we find something. And if you find anything, give me a call."

"Thank you."

Jasen walks him out, and I lie across the couch. I can't get the detective's words out of my head. He said there was evidence of rape. Could someone else have entered her home and raped her? If it wasn't Cooper who killed her, then why is he missing? "You must be tired," Jasen says when he returns to the living room. He sits beside me and places my legs across him. My head falls back, and my eyes close. "Get some sleep, baby" is the last thing I hear before I drift to sleep.

MORGAN: PRESENT DAY

It's been six weeks. Six weeks that I've been living as Monroe. Time has passed quickly. Week one, the week we swapped, the two weeks after that where I planned and held her funeral, and three more weeks after that where I put my home on the market and settled in quite nicely as my sister. I've had time. Plenty of time to come clean with him. Especially after we buried her. But as time passed on, so did my courage to tell the truth. Jasen is being extra attentive right now. And I'm welcoming it. I need it. There's a void without my sister. I feel like a piece of me is missing. We baked in the same womb. We were born just minutes apart. And as much as we argued, we loved each other, despite our differences. I can't get the image of her dead body out of my head. She appears in my dreams. Maybe she's trying to tell me something.

I could barely keep it together when Jasen and I met with the detective less than an hour ago. He came across something strange and wanted to speak with us about it. When we arrived, he slid the photo of my deceased sister across the table and asked us if we recognized a green emerald ring she was wearing. I have no idea where that ring came from. The detective explained further that the ring belonged to Cooper's grandmother. That it was a family heirloom. Simone wasn't even aware of it. How strange. Why would Cooper kill my sister and then leave without taking his grandmother's ring? A ring that is considered priceless. I couldn't pull my eyes away from the photo. I couldn't pull myself together seeing her spread out and covered in blood. The detective offered to speak with us another time. He said he understands how hard this is for me. But I had no words to respond. I was staring at the picture of my dead sister, wondering if there was any way I could have saved her. I was just about to answer the detective when I got the call from the doctor. The phone call telling me I'm pregnant.

I had suspected I was. I had missed my period, and the classic symptoms were there. So, I found a nearby doctor who was accepting new patients and made an appointment. I told her I had never visited an ob/gyn to avoid her wanting my previous medical history. I left Jasen to speak with the detective while I took the call, and then I sat in the waiting room and nervously bit my nails almost down to the meat. I stand when I see him walking towards me. He smiles when he grabs my hand.

"It's going to be okay. Let's go home."

Jasen types away on his laptop once we get home. He's been working nonstop since Cooper's absence. He dissolved Cooper's share of the business and made sure Simone got all of it. I haven't been able to help him much since my sister's death, so he plans to hire someone to help around the office at some point. I snack on a bag of pretzels as he types away. "I'm almost done," he says with his eyes glued to the screen.

"Take your time. I know…"

I can't finish the sentence. Because the bile has risen in my throat. My stomach churns, and I bolt to my feet, sprinting to the bathroom. I barely make it before spilling my guts into the toilet. Jasen is right behind me. "Are you alright?"

I can't answer him. I feel too nauseous to speak. He steps inside the bathroom and pulls my hair away from my face. "Sweetheart, are you sick?"

I flush the toilet and grab a nearby towel to wipe my mouth. I stand and make my way to the sink to brush my teeth. I watch him in the mirror behind me as I rigorously brush. I swish the toothpaste around, removing the taste of vomit. When I spit the toothpaste out, his eyes narrow with concern. "I'm calling the doctor."

"No."

He's stops and turns around. "I know you hate doctors, but I'm worried about you. You hardly ever get sick."

I grip the edge of the sink tightly when I face him. "Jasen, I'm not sick. I'm pregnant."

CHAPTER 14

JASEN

I'm speechless. I stand shell-shocked while she waits for me to respond. "Are you going to say something?"

"Are you sure?"

"Yes, I got the call today."

"How far along are you?"

"I haven't had my follow-up appointment yet, but I'm guessing around six weeks."

Worry crosses her face. "Are you upset?"

I shake my head. "No. I... I'm surprised. I didn't think you wanted kids."

She smiles. "I guess the universe thought otherwise."

"I guess so. How about you run a hot bath, and I'll go get you some ginger tea? It'll help with the nausea."

"Good idea. We'll talk more when you get back?"

"Yeah, definitely."

~

My head rests on the steering wheel, and I grip it tightly. I'm sitting in the parking lot of the grocery store, too anxious to drive. My adrenaline is pumping. I'm sweating. I can't breathe. My mind is spiraling out of control from the news I just received. My wife just told me she's pregnant. Only that can't be possible. My mind replays that awful day.

"How long will she need rest?"

The doctor takes her blood pressure again. "About six to eight weeks."

My leg shakes with nervousness. "And there's no other way to fix this?"

He reads the numbers on the monitor and removes it from her arm. Once he writes the numbers down, he turns to face me. "I know this isn't easy, Mr. Baker. But the fibroids could become cancerous if we wait too long. They're twice the size they were last time, and they'll keep growing. A hysterectomy is the only way to fix this."

I grab Monroe's hand. "Are you sure about this? What about us having a baby?"

She squeezes my hand. "I know you want kids. But I honestly don't want any, Jasen. And I'm tired of going through this every month. My periods are way too heavy, and the pain is getting worse. I need to do this."

Disappointment sweeps through me. "Are we all set?" the doctor asks.

"Yes," Monroe answers.

"Okay. Let's get you to the operating room. Mr. Baker, we'll let you know when she's all done."

Some small part of me thought she did it on purpose. To make sure that kids weren't in the cards for us. When we first found out she had fibroids, the doctor said we could try to conceive before we discussed a hysterectomy as an option. This way, we could at least have a baby before it was too late. But she didn't want that. When they wheeled Monroe out of surgery, I was overcome with sadness. I took her home and cared for her for over a month. The sadness intensified each day. I know the fibroids were out of her control, but I blamed her for it anyway. She knew I wanted kids. And she made sure that didn't happen. As time dragged on, I got over it. I considered adoption, but I knew she wouldn't go for it. So, I didn't bring it up. I came to grips that I would never be a father. I pushed the idea of fatherhood to the back of my mind. Until today. Today, I found out I'm going to be a father. The only difference is it won't be with my wife.

I return to the house with ginger tea and shortbread cookies. I don't feel any better than when I left the house. My blood is boiling. I feel like a fool. All this time? How did I not know?

"Jasen?"

I turn around and come face-to-face with the only logical explanation for all of this. I stare at the woman who holds the same eyes as my wife. The same skin tone. The same hair. She's wearing an oversized sweatshirt and a pair of pink leggings. My eyes drift to her belly. "Have a seat. I'll make your tea."

She sits at the table while I boil the water and place the tea bag inside of a mug. "Are you sure you're okay?"

"Yeah."

Once the water is boiling, I pour it in the mug. I drizzle a little honey inside, grab a spoon, and stir it up. I place it in front of her when I sit down. "Let it sit for a minute."

"Okay."

We're both quiet. She watches me with curiosity, and I cross my arms to compose myself. "I need you to start talking."

She appears confused. Such a good actress. No wonder she was able to pull it off. "About what?"

By now, I've lost all reason. She's playing with my intelligence. "You know goddamn well what I'm talking about, *Morgan.*"

She gasps, and her eyes go wide. "I…"

"Monroe couldn't have children. She had a hysterectomy two years ago. How long? How long did you two play this little game of yours?"

I've hit a nerve. A tear slides down her cheek, and her lip quivers. "Over a month."

I slam my fist down on the table, startling her enough to jump. I lean in, and my eyes sear into hers. I need her to see the pain in them. The anger. The betrayal. "We're going to sit here. And you're going to tell me every fucking detail from *A* to *Z*."

"I wanted to tell you."

"When?" I yell. "Before or after my wife was murdered?"

Her body shakes as she sobs. I stand up, grab some tissues—because what man allows a pregnant woman to cry?—and I hand them to her. "Get yourself together so you can talk."

I sit in silence for what seems like hours and watch the tears fall as she struggles to tell me what I need to hear. Finally, after the last tear has fallen, her red-rimmed eyes meet mine. "I didn't want to do this at first."

"But you did."

She nods.

"Why?"

"Monroe was having an affair. She said she was unhappy and needed time away to decide what she wanted to do. She asked me to swap with her for a weekend. At first, I didn't want to do it. I told her she was lucky to have you. I told her she was making a mistake. But she insisted on it. Finally, I agreed, and we switched places. That weekend turned into a week and..."

Her tears fall again. "She decided she couldn't do it. She couldn't return to her life, and she wanted to go away. We agreed to make the switch permanent."

"You two decided to live a lie. How could you two do something so reckless? Did you ever once think about the consequences of this? How it would affect Simone? Me?"

"Yes."

And they still went through with it. It's a punch to my gut. My wife deceived me. "All this time, I thought…" I try my best to shake the anger I'm feeling. Morgan is just as guilty in this, but she doesn't deserve one hundred percent of my wrath. "All this time, I thought my wife was changing for the better. I thought my marriage was doing better. I thought we were falling in love all over again. And the whole time, this was some fucking joke between you two?"

Her hand slides across the table to connect with mine, but I pull mine back quickly. Hurt flashes in her eyes. But it shouldn't —because she's partially at fault for this. The other person I need to blame is dead. "Who was she having an affair with?"

She doesn't answer me right away. But she doesn't have to. I connected the dots as soon as she told me Monroe was having an affair. How else would I explain my wife being murdered and my business partner going missing? "Cooper," she answers softly.

I shove to my feet. I walk over to the counter and place my hands at the edge of it. Sure, I connected the dots, but hearing the truth makes it worse. "How long?"

She shakes her head. "I don't know."

"You're lying."

"No. I'm not. I don't know. I hadn't spoken to Monroe in months because of the argument we had."

She's telling the truth. I had forgotten that the two of them weren't on speaking terms. "Did Simone know?"

"She suspected. She found text messages in Cooper's phone. Monroe was going to break it off with Cooper the day she was killed."

Stop it!

"Cooper must have killed her when she tried to leave him."

Shut up, please.

The more she speaks, the angrier I become. My emotions are conflicting. I'm angry at my wife, but she's not here for me to question her. To lash out at. She's dead. I'm suddenly hit with another emotion. Grief. It was my wife who was killed, not her sister. And I didn't get a proper goodbye. I wasn't close to Morgan. So, when I thought it was her who died, I was there for who I thought was my wife. I stepped up and helped with the arrangements. I held her while she sobbed in my arms. I was sad for her. And I did everything I could to help ease her pain. I felt sadness that I lost a sister-in-law. But that feeling is nowhere near compared to finding out that I've lost Monroe.

"Jasen, at first it was supposed to be a swap. But as I spent more time around you, I fell for you. I didn't know I would feel this way. I didn't know I would fall in love with you."

I take my arm and angrily knock the pitcher of orange juice to the floor. It crashes loudly and juice splatters everywhere. I breathe heavily with my eyes shut tightly. "She was your sister, Morgan. My wife is lying dead in the ground, and you're sitting here telling me you're in love with me?"

"I just want you to know that this is real for me."

I shake my head. "I can't do this shit right now."

She's out of her seat in a flash and in front of me. "I understand. You have a right to be angry. But I *never* wanted to hurt you."

"Hurt. You think I'm hurt? That's at the bottom of the list of things I'm feeling right now, Morgan. Fury and betrayal are at the top."

"I know."

I take a few steps back to distance myself from her. "You can't be here."

"But where am I supposed to go? I put my house up for sale."

I hold my hands up in surrender. "I know. I'm not kicking you out. I'm going to take the guest room until I figure this out."

"What about the baby?"

"Are you sure it's mine?"

She nods. "I hadn't been with anyone before you."

"Then I'll figure that out too."

I slept about an hour before I decided it was useless trying to sleep. I lie awake and stare at the ceiling, thinking about Monroe. How could she? I knew we were having problems, but I didn't think they were bad enough for her to go this far. Los Angeles is huge. You're talking millions of people. And she had to have an affair with my business partner. Typical, selfish Monroe. My thoughts shift to my time spent with Morgan. I was happy. The happiest I've been in a long time. But it was all a lie. Morgan pretended to be Monroe. And I missed all the signs. Now that the truth is out, I see that the signs were right under my nose. Her doing dishes by hand. Apologizing. Refusing expensive gifts. Now it all makes sense. Monroe would have *never* done any of that. But instead of paying more attention, I was caught up in accepting the new and improved her. I knew Monroe could be brutal. I knew she could be selfish. I knew she was the type of person to go above and beyond to get what she wanted. But this? I never imagined she'd do something so fucked-up like this. Because of her selfishness, she's dead and her sister is pregnant with my baby.

I should be happy at the thought of fatherhood. And a piece of me is happy. I've wanted to be a father since the day I married her. But not this way. Not by unknowingly having sex with my sister-in-law. I'm at war with myself. She could still have an abortion at six weeks, but is that something she would want to do? Is it something I would want her to do? It's a question I can't answer. On one hand, I think this situation is too complicated and fucked-up to bring an innocent life into. On the other hand, the baby is just that, an innocent life. It didn't ask to be conceived. I'm not thinking clearly right now, and I don't want to make decisions based on impulse. I know I'll regret it if I do. There's a soft knock at the door. I glance at the clock. It's 6:00 a.m. The door opens slowly, and Morgan pokes her head in. "I was going to make some coffee."

I sit up. "I don't think it's safe for you to drink coffee with the baby?"

She nods. "Then I'll make some for you."

"Thanks. But I'll make it myself."

I grab my cell phone from the nightstand and scroll through emails. I can't look at her right now.

"I have my first doctor's appointment this morning. I'd like for you to be there, but I understand if you don't want to come."

I stop scrolling. "What time?"

"10:00 a.m."

I turn to face her. "I'll go."

We're dressed and ready to go when the doorbell rings. I open the door, and my mouth drops open. "Simone."

"Hi, Jasen. Is now a good time?"

It's not a good time at all. Not only do Morgan and I have an appointment to get to, but I'm not in the mood to offer my sympathy to a grieving widow whose husband was fucking my wife. But I step aside and let her in. "Sure, come in."

I lead her to the living room and offer her a seat. "I'm sorry to just drop by like this, but as you can imagine, this has been hard to deal with."

I nod. "I've been meaning to come by, Simone, but with the funeral and dealing with the detective on the case—"

"I know," she interrupts.

"Did you get the check I mailed you? It's Cooper's share of the business. Every cent of it."

"Yes. Thank you."

I take a seat beside her on the couch. "I know it's a lot. And I'm sorry I didn't come by to see you. How are you holding up?"

Her expression changes as soon as I ask. The tears swell, and she looks like she's about to cry. She shakes her head instead. "I don't know. It hurts to know that Cooper could have done such a horrible thing."

"I know."

She turns to face me. "I just can't believe it."

"Me either."

"I keep waiting by the phone, thinking he'll call and explain all of this."

"Do you have any idea where he could be?"

"No. And it doesn't look like the police know either. I hope they find him. I need answers, Jasen. I need to know why."

"I'm sorry, Simone."

It's the second time I've said it, but it's all I can offer her right now. An apology. An apology for my wife's role in the situation.

"I'm ready. Sorry, I had to—" Morgan stops in her tracks. Simone and I both shoot to our feet.

"Honey, you remember Simone."

"Yes, of course." She walks forward and pulls Simone in tightly for a hug. "I'm so sorry."

Simone's eyes go wide as she slowly raises her arms to hug Morgan back. They stay that way for a second before they pull away. "If you need anything, please let us know."

Simone nods. "I'm sorry about your sister.

Morgan smiles. "You have nothing to be sorry about."

"The detective said you spoke to her that day. Did she say anything? Anything at all?"

"No. She didn't."

Simone accepts her answer. "Well, I guess I better get going. I just wanted to come by and formally offer my condolences for... what was your sister's name again?"

"Morgan."

"I wanted to offer my condolences for Morgan and to see how the two of you are holding up."

"Thank you for dropping by."

We walk Simone to the door. "You have my number. Promise you'll call if you need anything?"

"Yeah, I promise."

She's almost out the door when she stops. "Will you let me know if you hear from Cooper?"

"Of course."

She nods before she walks down the steps and towards her car. Morgan and I watch from the doorway. "That poor woman. I can only imagine how hard this is for her."

I crane my neck to watch Simone start her car. "Yeah, she's hurting, that's for sure." We stand in silence as we watch Simone drive away. When she's out of sight, I turn to face her. "Ready?"

"Yeah, let's go."

CHAPTER 15

JASEN

I allowed the music to play through the speakers the entire ride to the doctor's office. And not the same doctor Monroe saw. Turns out Morgan found a new doctor. The doctor just finished an internal exam where she was lying with her knees up and her feet in stirrups. Now, she's lying flat on her back on the exam table. The doctor squirts some type of jelly on her stomach and places a device on it. "There it is," she says as she points to the screen with her finger. I squint hard but still have no idea how she can identify that tiny object as a baby. Morgan's face lights up as she watches the screen. "You're about six weeks along. Would you like to hear the heartbeat?"

She turns her head to face me. Her eyes ask, *Is this what I want?* I nod in agreement. She turns to face the doctor again. "Yes."

The doctor presses a few buttons. There are some strange noises, but then... we hear it. Thump, thump, thump. I stand to my feet and move closer to the screen as I hear the baby's heartbeat. *My* baby's heartbeat. I can't explain what I'm feeling right now. It's something I've never felt before. My heart swells with this new and indescribable feeling. The corners of my mouth curve upward as I watch and listen to the life I helped create. "The heartbeat is strong. But there is something I'm a little concerned about."

My mouth curves downward quickly. "Is something wrong?' I ask.

She presses a few buttons, and the sound stops. She takes some napkins and wipes away the gel on Morgan's belly. When she's done, she places her hands on her hips. "Your cervix should be one hundred percent closed at this point. But it's not. Seems you're slightly dilated, and I'm going to have to put you on bed rest."

"Am I at risk of losing the baby?" Panic crosses Morgan's face. I go to her side and grab her hand. I don't know what makes me do it, but I do. I can only imagine how scary this must be for her.

"We're not panicking yet. But we need to be cautious. I need you off your feet as much as possible. Eat healthy. And no stress."

Morgan nods but is clearly concerned. "I'll make sure she's off her feet, Doc."

Before this moment, I considered asking Morgan to take her house off the market. I figured it was best for her to go back to Philadelphia; we could work out the logistics of co-parenting later. But after hearing the doctor's orders, there's no way I can do that. She's been ordered to bed rest. Which means she's going to need my help. The doctor smiles. "That's good to hear. I'll be back with more instructions, and you'll be all set to go home."

When she leaves the room, I let go of Morgan's hand. "Jasen, are you sure about this? I can do this on my own."

"I'm sure. You're carrying my baby, Morgan. The least I can do is help."

∼

After I get Morgan settled on the couch, I bring her a cup of ginger tea. She's still feeling a little nauseous from the morning sickness. I take a seat next to her. "I think we should talk about how we're going to move forward."

She takes a sip of her tea. "Okay."

"This isn't a fairy tale, Morgan. We're not going to fall in love and ride into the sunset. You're my wife's sister who conned her way into my life and got pregnant."

She looks like I just slapped her. "I'm not trying to upset you," I continue. But it's important that I be up-front with where I stand on this."

"I get it."

"You'll stay here. I'll work from home as much as I can, and the days I need to be at the office, I'll hire a nurse."

"I don't think that's necessary."

"It is for me. I need someone here who can look after you in case something happens. I don't want you home alone."

"Okay."

"I'm doing this because I'm going to be a father. I may not agree with how it happened, but it happened. I'm doing what's best for our child."

"You said we won't fall in love. It's too late for me. I've fallen in love with you."

"And I fell in love with who I thought was my wife."

"No. You fell in love with me. You and I both know Monroe would never have made that much of an effort."

"No, Morgan. I *don't* know. I won't get to find out what effort she would have made because guess what? You agreed to swap lives with her, and now she's dead."

"But I…"

I sense her getting upset. She's supposed to remain stress-free, and I refuse to be the cause of any anxiety she feels. I hold my hands up. "Listen, I'm sorry. I don't want to cause you any stress. I'm just dealing with a lot right now."

"I'm sorry, Jasen. I really am. It may not seem like it, but I miss her too."

I exhale loudly. "I know you do."

I can't deny that she doesn't miss Monroe. Those were real tears she shed for her sister. The pain in her eyes was real. I know without a doubt that she grieved her sister's death. "There's something else we need to discuss."

"What is it?"

"We need to tell Detective Henby."

Her eyes go wide. "We can't."

"We have to, Morgan. He needs to know about Cooper and Monroe. He needs to know the truth so he can close this case properly."

"But I lied. I could get in trouble, Jasen. I falsely identified her as me. I knew about her and Cooper having an affair. I could go to jail."

A war wages in my mind. She's right. She lied to a detective. She withheld information. They could charge her. And she would go to jail. While pregnant with my child. But what about Monroe? She deserves to have her murderer brought to justice. And that can't happen if the detective doesn't have all the facts. "Morgan, this is my wife we're talking about. Your sister. Don't you want to see her killer brought to justice?"

"Of course I do."

"Then we have to tell the truth regardless of the circumstances. The detective has no clue how to solve this case. This will help him."

She shakes her head. "I can't risk it right now, Jasen. Not while I'm pregnant. I won't get the kind of medical care I need in a prison cell."

Her voice has risen. It's panicked. She's frightened. "Okay.

But after the baby is born, we tell the truth. No more lies, Morgan."

"Okay. No more lies."

She sits back with relief, and I watch her sip her tea. "Just tell me one more thing," I ask.

"Anything."

"Was she ever coming back?"

She hesitates for a second. "I don't think so."

"None of this bothers you. You don't feel bad about sleeping with your sister's husband and carrying his baby. Isn't that against sister code or something?"

She giggles. "Yeah. It is. But she broke the sister code first."

I cock my head to the side with curiosity. "What do you mean by that?"

She smiles behind her cup of tea. "Jasen, I liked you first."

MORGAN

I felt a huge weight lifted off me as soon as the truth came out. The longer I pretended to be Monroe, the harder it became to admit the truth to Jasen. Even though Monroe and I agreed that our plan was what was best for all of us, I knew deep down that Jasen didn't deserve to be lied to. So, I'm glad he finally found out. Because I'm not sure if I would've ever admitted the truth if he didn't. I had no idea Monroe had a hysterectomy. I wonder why she didn't tell me about it. At one time, we told each other everything. Or so I thought.

"What are you talking about?"

"Do you remember that day? The day Monroe approached you in the cafeteria?"

"Yeah. She asked me for my phone number."

"Right. Well, it was supposed to be for me. I had this huge crush on you, but I was shy. She said she would get your number for me."

He shakes his head. "She never mentioned you."

"I know. She got it for herself, and then you two started dating. I couldn't believe she would hurt me like that. But she did. It was torture watching you two at school together. It was worse when you came to the house to pick her up or visit her. She rubbed it in my face too. She knew it bothered me."

"I never knew that."

"It's not your fault. But that's the reason I never came to visit. I just couldn't do it."

He looks uncomfortable. "That was a long time ago, Morgan. We were teenagers."

"I know."

"Is that why you and Monroe had a strained relationship?"

"No. Our relationship is... *was* complicated. There would be periods of time when we were stuck together like glue. Times when we told each other everything. Times where she was my best friend. But then she would do or say something to hurt me, and we would stop speaking to each other. Our relationship was off and on most of the time."

"Yeah, I got that impression. I always wondered why you didn't come around more. I mean, you two were twins. So, is that why you're telling me everything about her? Is that why you're spilling her secrets? Was this some sort of payback?"

"No. I'm telling you the truth because you're a good man, Jasen. You deserve to hear the truth. And because it's the right thing to do. If we're going to co-parent, it's important you know everything. And we agreed... no more secrets."

He rubs the back of his neck with frustration. "What do you want to happen here, Morgan?"

My answers are on the tip of my tongue. I want him. I want to start over. I want us to be a family. But I don't tell him this. It's too soon. He's still grieving Monroe. We both are. "I want to do what's best for our baby."

"Good. Then we're both in agreement."

~

We fell asleep on the couch last night. I woke up early and went upstairs to take a hot shower. My boobs itch like crazy, and the hot water is the only thing that seems to soothe them. I step out of the shower, dry myself off, and wrap the towel around me. I freeze when I enter the bedroom. Jasen's standing in front of the dresser, wearing nothing but a pair of gym shorts. His eyes rake my body before he quickly averts them. "I needed some clean clothes."

I try my best not to stare at his erection. But it's hard to miss. My eyes jump to his when he closes the drawer. "I was going to head downstairs to make breakfast once I get dressed. Would you like something?"

"No, thank you. I'm gonna shower, then head down to the office to get some work done."

"Oh. Okay."

"You shouldn't be on your feet anyway. I'll call Otis this morning."

"Jasen, I'm fine. I don't think cooking is that big of a deal."

"I beg to differ. I'm not taking any chances, Morgan."

He walks out the room, and I follow him. "You can't expect me to stay in bed all day."

He turns around and runs his hand down his face with frustration. "You heard the doctor. Are you really arguing with me about this?"

I relax a little because he's right. The doctor said to stay off my feet as much as possible. But still, I don't like it. "No. You're right."

He walks away and yells over his shoulder, "If you need me, call me."

JASEN

This is harder than I expected it to be. I'm trying to be hospitable to Morgan. But how can you be hospitable to a woman you've slept with? Seeing her just now in nothing but a towel made me want to rip it off her. I'm angry with her. So angry. But my body remembers how she felt. My mind remembers how she's made me feel the past six weeks. And as much as I try to forget, I can't. She looked stunning this morning. Her skin was glowing with tiny beads of water dripping down her neck. I could see the firmness of her breasts through the towel. And my dick got hard at the sight of it hugging her curves. I know what's under it. I know what she felt like. And as sick as it sounds, I wanted her. What kind of person am I to lust after my own sister-in-law? A horrible one. Which is why I got away quickly. I'm reading a client's file when there's a knock at the door. The door opens, and Morgan steps in with a tray of food. I place the folder down and stand up. I grab the tray from her and place it on my desk. "And I thought your sister was stubborn. It seems neither of you listen."

"Actually, Otis brought it down for me. He didn't hand it to me until after I knocked. I wanted to be the one to bring you breakfast."

"Thank you. But you didn't have to do this. I'm not really hungry."

"Well, your body needs food, whether you want it or not. You can't work on an empty stomach."

My stomach chooses that exact moment to growl, and she giggles. "See?"

"Thank you for the food."

"You're welcome. Do you need help with anything?"

"No. I'm fine."

"Okay. Well, let me know if you do. It'll be nice to have something to occupy my time."

"I'll keep that in mind."

She waits around for a few moments before she grabs the doorknob. "Alright, I'll see you later."

"Okay. See you later."

The door closes, and relief sweeps through me. How can she be so calm and normal when I'm doing somersaults inside? One minute, I want to scream at her, and the next, I want to fuck her. I don't trust myself around her right now. I don't want to cause her any stress. But I also don't want to cross the line with her again. Ever. The best thing for me to do is be neutral. I need to be emotionless around her. Limit my interaction with her. This way, there are no mixed signals and I don't take my anger out on her. She'll thank me later. She'll understand why it must be this way. She'll see that I did this to protect us both. She said she wants to do what's best for the baby, and that is what I'm doing. So, why do I feel so bad for doing it?

CHAPTER 16

JASEN

I've been avoiding Morgan for over a week now. I brought some clothes and toiletries into the guest room so we don't have another repeat of me walking in after she's showered. I try to grab breakfast on the way to the office. And if I work from home, I've told Otis to bring it to me. I'm not comfortable with Morgan carrying anything. Even if it's for a minute. I eat my dinner in the guest room or in my office if I'm working late. I check on her throughout the day by text. I purchased a new phone for her and placed Monroe's in the safe. It was weird texting my wife's number knowing she's dead. I'm in the kitchen grabbing a protein bar when Morgan walks in. Shit! I thought she was taking a nap. "Hey."

She's wearing a pair of purple sweats that cling to her hips and a pink tank top that barely covers the swell of her breasts. Her face is radiant, and her hair is in a ponytail. "Hey. How are you feeling?"

She grabs a banana from the fruit tray. "Pretty good. No morning sickness today. I'm really tired though."

"That's good to hear."

She peels the banana and takes a bite. Jesus help me. The way her lips wrap around it make me think sinful things. "I haven't seen you much."

"Yeah, got some new clients, so I've been busy. I'm either at the office or working downstairs."

"Oh."

She takes another bite, and I almost moan at the sight. "I'll be working from home today, if you need me."

I walk away, but when I walk past her, she stops me. She places her hand on my arm, and it's like fireworks go off inside. "Jasen. How long are you going to do this?"

"Do what?"

"Blame me. Come on. I know you've been avoiding me."

"I'm working."

"I know you're angry. But I can't live like this." Tears swell in her eyes. "I can't be here knowing you hate me." Her voice cracks as she says it. Cracking my heart with it. She thinks I hate her. It's far from the truth. I hate what she and Monroe did. But I don't hate her. Or Monroe. Her tears spill over, and she releases my arm. "I'm going to go lie down."

She flees the kitchen quickly before I have a chance to stop her.

I enter the bedroom carefully. When she hears me come in, she wipes away her tears. "I'm okay," she says convincingly.

I sit beside her. "No. You're not."

"I wish I could get you to understand that I never meant to hurt you. If I could have done things differently..."

I place my hand over hers, hoping to make her feel better. Only it does the opposite. It makes *me* feel. "I don't hate you. This is hard for me, Morgan. I don't know how to feel around you. I'm grieving my wife. I'm angry about what you two did. And I'm conflicted about you."

"Me?"

"Yeah. The time we spent together, you made me feel something again. Something I can't forget, no matter how much I try. It feels like I'm betraying Monroe by feeling the way I do. But I guess she never really cared anyway."

She inches closer to me. "It wasn't her fault, Jasen. I'm not excusing what she did. But Monroe had issues. Issues neither of us could help her with. She said herself she thought something was wrong with her. There was more to it than her having an affair. I think she did love you. I just don't think she was meant to settle down. With anyone."

"Yeah, well, it would have been nice to know that *before* we got married."

"I don't think she knew it then."

I turn to face her. "I'm sorry for the way I've been acting. I've been an ass, and you deserve better."

"I hate knowing that we hurt you."

"There's nothing I can do about that now. But let's start over, okay?"

"I'd like that."

"Good. I want you to be comfortable here. Happy here. You should have a stress-free pregnancy."

She smiles. "Thank you."

Our hands still touch. She's close enough for me to smell the banana on her breath. Her round doe eyes watch me intensely. A force pulls me to her. My mind tells me to resist, but my body doesn't get the message. I press my lips against hers and wrap my hand around her waist. Her tongue dances with mine, and her breasts smash against my chest. I want to strip her naked. But I can't go there. I suddenly realize what we're doing, and I pull away. She doesn't speak. Her hand touches her lips that were just pressed against mine. I stand and adjust my pants. "I, ahh... I have a lot of work to catch up on. I'll see you later."

L.R. JACKSON

MORGAN

His kiss leaves me breathless. Wanting for more. It was a reminder of just how much I missed his touch. I wanted him to undress me. Make love to me. I wanted to tear his clothes off. But I knew if I became too aggressive, it would scare him away. So, I waited. Waited for him to make the first move. Only he didn't. He pulled his lips away with a look of regret before he bolted downstairs to avoid me again. I know why I'm still here. Living in his house. I know what our agreement was. But I can't help myself. I miss him so much, and it's killing me to be so close to him yet so far away. Every time I see him, I want my lips on his. My body craves his when I'm alone in my bed at night. I want to respect the boundaries he's put in place. I want to give him the space he needs to heal. But I feel like I'm going mad in the process. My fingers still touch my lips. It's like I'm trying to prove to myself that the kiss was real.

I stand to my feet. They move swiftly before I have a chance to talk myself out of it. I swing the bedroom door open. Sprint down the hall and down the steps. I breeze past the kitchen, past the dining room and the living room. I tread lightly down the stairs and stop when I arrive in front of Jasen's home office. I take a few minutes to let my heartbeat calm. It's beating so fast, it's scaring me. When I gather my composure, I knock softly. I turn the knob before he can open the door, and I step inside. He's on a call. He raises an eyebrow when I step in front of him. "I'll call you back." He stands. "Are you okay?"

Concern stretches across his face as he waits for an answer. The answer is no. I'm not okay. But not in the way he's asking. Physically, I feel fine. Great since the morning sickness has started to subside. But mentally and emotionally, I'm a wreck. So, I stick to my promise. No more lies. "No. I need you."

I wrap my arms around his neck and pull him to me, planting my lips on his. He resists at first. But only for a second before he pulls me in tighter. I moan as his hands slide under the tank top I'm wearing. I'm not wearing a bra. I haven't needed one since I found out I was pregnant. He kisses my neck as his fingers circle my nipples. "I need you, Jasen. Please."

I'm borderline begging for him. I'm desperate for him. He releases me, and I almost think he's going to kick me out of his office. But he doesn't. He pulls my shirt over my head. He undresses me in what feels like seconds, then undresses himself. He lies me down on the plush leather couch and hovers over me. He stares into my eyes as he eases inside of me. He pauses. "Are you sure?"

"Yes. Don't stop."

Sex with Jasen is amazing. But sex with him while pregnancy hormones are raging through my body is outstanding. He drives me crazy with his strokes. I moan loudly as he gently grabs a fistful of my hair. "I know this is wrong," he says in between strokes. "But it doesn't feel that way."

"Nothing about this feels wrong."

He grabs the arm of the couch and slightly raises himself up. His eyes bore into mine as he makes love to me. "It's been so long. Tell me it was real, Morgan."

Tears gather in my eyes. "It was real, Jasen. All of it."

His fingers lock with mine as he takes me over the edge, and I scream with ecstasy. He squeezes my fingers tightly as he groans and spills inside me. He doesn't move for a few minutes. "Morgan."

My heart squeezes tightly. He regrets it. "Please don't say it, Jasen."

He slides out of my gently and smiles. "I was only going to ask if I hurt you. Or the baby."

Relief sweeps through me. I shake my head. "No. We're both fine."

After Jasen and I made love, I expected him to shut me out again. But he didn't. He cleaned me up. Asked me if I was okay repeatedly. And kissed me before telling me he had a call he had to make. I spent the rest of day reading pregnancy magazines and thinking of names for the baby. It's evening time now, and Otis prepared a meal at my request. I was craving fried red snapper, mac 'n' cheese, and fresh cabbage. Jasen walks in just as I pour a little hot sauce on my fish. "Should you be eating spicy food?"

"The doctor didn't say otherwise."

"Oh."

He grabs a plate of food, and instead of taking it back to his office, he sits across from me at the table. "This smells good."

"I know. Otis really outdid himself."

We both dig in, and the food tastes as good as it smells. I chew with happiness as the food satisfies my cravings. "I spoke with Detective Henby this afternoon."

"Any news on Cooper?"

"No. They still haven't found him. They're thinking of getting the feds involved."

I stop chewing. "Do you think they'll figure out what we've done?"

Panic soars through my entire body. The FBI don't play around. If anyone can figure out what I've done, it's them. Jasen sets his fork down. "Not if I can help it."

"How can you be so sure?"

"Morgan, I'm going to do whatever I can to protect you and our baby."

CHAPTER 17

MORGAN

Things have shifted between Jasen and me the past few weeks. We talk more. We have dinner together every night, and he no longer sleeps in the guest room. We're making the effort to make our situation as normal as it can be. I sense he still grieves Monroe. I can tell he's still upset about what we did. But he deals with it in his own way. Some nights, he sits on the patio with a glass of whiskey, staring out at the LA lights. It's his time to reflect. His time to think. I never bother him. I don't force him to tell me what's on his mind. I have my own demons I'm battling. As much as I love Jasen, I can't help but carry the guilt of my sister's death. I can't help but feel regret about swapping with her. I regret hurting Jasen. The only thing that keeps me happy is the baby I'm carrying. I lay my hand across my belly and visualize how it will look. Will it be a boy? A girl? I'm excited to meet him or her. My mind shifts to all the preparation that needs to be done before the baby gets here. I haven't purchased one bottle or blanket. I haven't even figured out where it will sleep.

I shoot to my feet as I suddenly think about the empty bedroom down the hall. Jasen was going to turn it into a gym. But I have other things in mind. I open the door and walk inside. It's huge in size, like all the rooms in this house. It has a beautiful bay window, a cathedral ceiling, and wall-to-wall plush carpet. It's perfect. I grow more excited as I think about how I want to decorate the room. I pull the phone out of my pocket and call Jasen. "Hey."

"I want to decorate the baby's room."

"Which room did you pick?"

"The room you were going to turn into a gym."

"Oh, good choice."

"Yeah. I think so too. I'll need paint. I need to buy a bassinet. A rocking chair—"

"Whoa, calm down. You're not painting anything. Text me everything you need. I'll have our maintenance guy come and paint. And I'll order the deliveries for everything else."

"But that takes away the fun of shopping for the baby. I thought we could go to Target. We could make a day of it."

"Morgan…"

I sigh loudly. "Okay. I know. I shouldn't be on my feet. But just for the record, this sucks!"

"I'll help you decorate. We can make a day of it, then."

"Deal. It's going to be so much fun."

JASEN

When I said I would help Morgan decorate the baby's room, it sounded good at the time. My maintenance guy painted the room a few days ago. She opted for a unisex color. Mint green. After she sent me a three-page list of all the things she needed, I had it delivered. I'm currently standing here surrounded by boxes of bottles, bibs, baby clothes, and diapers. I have my drill in hand, squinting at page two of the directions on how to put the crib together. I'm sweating. I'm nervous. My child will be sleeping in this. One wrong screw, and my baby can fall to its death. I can't fuck this up. "I don't understand. There should be one last screw that goes right here." I point to the remaining hole. Morgan walks over. "Hmmm. You're right."

I turn around to grab the bag that the pieces came in and feel something hard under my foot. I lift my leg up, and there it is. The missing screw. She places her hands on her hips. "Looks like we found it."

I pick it up, toss the directions, and drill the last screw in. I take a step back and look at my work. "That's it."

Morgan joins me at my side. She places her hand on the mahogany crib and beams. "It's perfect."

I grab the mattress and place it snugly inside. Morgan follows behind with the sheet and blanket. We did it. The room is painted. The crib is complete. The rocking chair sits in the corner. And the toy chest is filled with enough toys to last a life-time. I know she went overboard. But I don't care. Our baby will be spoiled to pieces, and I can't wait. She looks around the room. "It's exactly the way I imagined it. Thank you."

I wrap my arm around her. "I'm excited about being a father."

"You are?"

"Yes, I am. Morgan, we can't deny that this is a complicated situation. We have a long road ahead of us, but..." I think care-fully about what I'm about to say next. "But I want to get through it, together."

Confusion crosses her face. "Are you saying we'll get through it together as parents or..."

"I'm saying whatever happens, happens. Monroe's betrayal is still fresh. But I can't deny that things weren't right with us for a long time. We loved each other, but we fell out of love with each other years ago. I think we just became comfortable with each other. And in some weird way, she was right. We weren't compatible. I tried to make her into someone she wasn't. Morgan, the weeks I spent with you... I can't shake how you made me feel. I loved Monroe. But she never made me feel the way you do."

"Jasen, what are you saying?" she asks in almost a whisper.

"I don't want to force anything between us just because of the baby. But I won't deny my feelings anymore. I want to move forward as a family. There are a thousand reasons why we shouldn't be together, Morgan. But I don't care about any of them."

This has weighed heavily on my mind the past few weeks. And the more I thought about it, the more I came to the conclusion that maybe fate has given me everything I ever wanted in some sick way. I valued my marriage. I was loyal to Monroe. I tried my hardest to make us work. I did everything I could to make her happy. But it wasn't enough. I'm tired of blaming myself for our failed marriage. For her death. I've got to let the weight of it go if I have any chance of being happy. I'm standing in front of a woman who sees me for who I am. A woman who accepts me for who I am. A woman who desires nothing more from me than love. It's the little things that matter to Morgan. She makes me feel good enough for her. Maybe it wasn't meant for Monroe and me. Maybe I chose the wrong girl all those years ago. I may never know why Monroe treated me the way that she did. I may never know why she was so unhappy. But should I torture myself by trying to find the answers? Or should I accept what's right in front of me? Her eyes blink rapidly "Are you sure about this?"

I nod. "I'm sure."

The truth is that I'm not one hundred percent sure that I'm doing the right thing. But I'm taking a leapt of faith that I am. I'm trusting my instinct when it's telling me that this is what's best for our baby. Best for us. My gut is telling me that Morgan's feelings for me are real. I felt them. I still do feel them. "Jasen, I don't know what to say."

"Is this what you want?"

"More than anything."

"Then there's nothing left to say."

CHAPTER 18

MORGAN

We're going to be a family. Me, Jasen, and our baby. I hum to myself as I place the last stuffed animal into the toy chest. Jasen went to the office for a few hours, and I've been in the baby's room all morning, just because. I like the excitement I feel when I'm in here. I dream about what kind of mother I'll be. What will I tell our baby about Monroe? It's going to be a difficult conversation for sure, but Jasen and I agreed that we won't hide the truth about how we conceived. I have a seat in the rocking chair and place my hand on my belly. I stop humming and close my eyes, allowing my thoughts to roam in the silence. That's when I hear it. The sound of a click. My eyes pop open, and I freeze. I stay completely still as Simone points the gun in my face.

"Don't you move."

"Simone..."

"Shut up. You thought you could sleep with my husband and get away with it. You think I would let him leave me?"

"No. You have it all wrong."

She shoves the gun closer. "I said shut up." I remain quiet

while I let her finish. "He should've listened to me. He should've stayed home. But he didn't. He came home that morning. I knew something was wrong, but he wouldn't talk to me. He shut me out like he always did. I told him I thought we were going to talk and work things out. Only he came home to tell me he was going to leave me. For you."

I shake my head. "I'm not..."

"Don't say another word." I raise my hands in surrender. "I begged him to stay, but he packed a suitcase. He said he wasn't happy with me and wanted to be with you. I cried. I told him I would do whatever he wanted if he stayed. But he left. And I followed him. I saw him come here. He went inside the house, and I waited. When I saw your housekeeper leave, I went inside. I heard voices upstairs and snuck up them slowly. I saw the suitcases packed. I thought you guys were running away together. I didn't know they weren't yours. I didn't know that your sister was visiting."

"Simone," I speak slowly. "What did you do?"

"I had to make it look like Cooper killed her. I made him place the emerald ring on her finger. I put my gun against his head and made him stab her. Then I shot him."

"You killed them both."

"He tried to make me seem like I was crazy. That I was making up stories about him having affairs. But I knew. I knew about every single one of them. You weren't the only one."

"What did you do with the body?"

"I dragged him out of the house and into the car. I went back inside, cleaned up his blood, then I buried him and both of their cell phones in our backyard. That way, I can be close to him, you know."

"Simone. You've got it all wrong."

"I said shut up, Monroe. I may be sorry about killing your sister, but I won't be sorry about killing you."

"Simone, listen to me carefully. The person you killed *was* Monroe. I'm Morgan. She asked me to switch places with her."

"You're lying. The detectives said I killed your sister. Morgan."

"Because we switched identification. I didn't tell the cops the truth."

"I don't believe you."

"I can prove it."

"How?"

"I still have Monroe's phone."

She thinks for a second before she pushes the gun against my forehead. "If you try anything sneaky, I'll kill you."

I nod. She allows me to stand and walk in front of her. She pushes the gun into my back. I walk slowly to our bedroom and open the safe where Jasen keeps Monroe's old cell phone. I power it on and unlock it. Then I hand it to her. "Just read our messages and see for yourself."

She snatches the phone out of my hand and scrolls through the messages exchanged between Monroe and me. She's quiet as she reads them, but I feel the gun slowly slipping away. I've got to get away from her. I can't allow her to harm my baby. "See, I'm telling the truth."

"Not so fast. You *helped* her go away for a weekend with my husband?"

She's got me there. "I didn't know he was married at first."

"Bullshit. You're just as bad as your whore of a sister. Both of you should rot in hell for what you did."

"Us? You *murdered* them, Simone. If anyone is going to hell, it's you."

I regret saying it as soon as it comes out. She comes around my front and points the gun at my belly. "Please, Simone. I'm sorry."

Her eyes are sagging, like she hasn't slept in weeks. "He was the love of my life. And she took him from me."

"You don't have to do this." I try my best to reason with her. She's holding the gun; therefore, she has the power.

"Yes, I do. I might have already killed Monroe, but you're just as much to blame for this as she is."

I no longer reason with her. I take a chance and try to get away for the sake of my baby. I grab her arm and wrestle with her for the gun. She's strong. But I feel myself getting stronger, terrified for my baby. I find myself taking control. My finger finds the trigger. I angle the gun so it's pointing at her, and I squeeze. She somehow gains enough strength to turn the gun back towards me and smiles right before she squeezes the trigger.

CHAPTER 19

JASEN

I arrived home about ten minutes ago and decided to pour myself a glass of water before checking on Morgan. Just as I take a sip, the sound of two gunshots rings through the air. The glass slips from my fingers, and I run up the stairs. "Morgan!"

I call for her frantically as I run through the hallway, checking inside each bedroom. When I reach the master bedroom, I stop. I panic at the sight before me. Morgan is lying on the floor. Simone is lying across from her. Blood is splattered on them both. I rush to Morgan's side and grab her hand. "Morgan. Baby."

She squeezes my hand. "Jasen."

I pull my phone out of my pocket and dial 911. I give my address and end the call. "It's going to be okay. The ambulance will be here soon."

"I... I'm sorry."

"Shhh, don't try to talk."

"Simone. She... she killed..."

She doesn't finish her sentence, but I don't care. What she

needs to tell me doesn't matter. The only thing that matters right now is that she's going to be okay. "Stay with me, baby. You're going to get through this."

"I love you."

"Morgan, stay with me."

Her eyes flutter open and closed, and I'm not sure if she hears me. "Hang on, baby. You can't leave me. I need you and the baby."

She doesn't respond, and her hand goes limp inside of mine. I shake her. "Morgan. Baby." She still doesn't respond. No. I can't lose her. I just found her. My body shakes as I lean over her, soaking her in my tears. "Morgan. I love you." But there's no response. The only thing I hear is the sound of the ambulance in the background.

EPILOGUE

JASEN

It's five in the morning, and I'm wide-awake. Like I have been for the past three months. I tiptoe down the hallway and enter the bedroom slowly. I lean over and smile when I see them fast asleep. It's becoming a habit for me. Watching my babies sleep in the middle of the night. I'm fascinated by them and can't believe that they're mine. Austin stirs first before he pops his brown eyes open. I scoop him up and rock him gently. "Shh, let's not wake your sister up, bud."

Alexis chooses that exact moment to start crying. I walk over to her crib and rock it gently. "Shh, it's okay, sweetheart, Daddy's here."

The door creaks open, and Morgan pads across the floor. "Did you wake them up again?"

I turn around to face her. "Nope."

She bends over and scoops up Alexis. "I don't believe you."

She sits in the rocking chair and removes the top of her nightgown. Alexis latches on and feeds hungrily. I smile at the sight. "What?" she asks after she yawns.

"I love watching you feed them."

"You love watching me feed them, or you love watching my boobs?"

I chuckle. "Both."

I thought I had lost her the day she got shot. But I didn't. She spent a week in the hospital after they removed the bullet from her shoulder. She explained to the detective what had happened that day. That Simone admitted to the killings. They were able to dig up Cooper's body from their backyard. She also admitted the truth. About everything. The detective watched us with wonder as Morgan told him about what she and Monroe had done. I was scared shitless. I thought he would arrest her on the spot. But he didn't. He tucked the notebook in his pocket. Looked between the both of us and told us life is too short. We were given a second chance, and we shouldn't take it for granted. I have no idea why he didn't report us. But I didn't dwell on it. Because he was right. Life is short. And I will never take it for granted again. We went home, and she recovered for the rest of her pregnancy. I took some time off work. Hell, I can afford it. We grew closer. And by the end of her pregnancy, I fell madly in love with her. I asked her to marry me, and she happily said yes. We wanted to be married before our babies were born, and she didn't want the hassle of a wedding while she was seven months pregnant. So, we had a priest conduct the ceremony in our home with my mother and Anthony in attendance.

Austin falls back asleep, and so does Alexis. We carefully place them back in their cribs and stand over them for a few minutes watching them settle in. The twins are identical. Both have a head full of curly hair and brown eyes. I was thankful to have a boy and girl. I don't need any repeats of that shit Monroe and Morgan pulled. But then again, it worked out for the best. Because it gave me Morgan. It gave me our babies. Once they're sound asleep, she smiles. "Perfect."

I grab her hand and turn to her. "You sure are."

MORGAN

I pull the turkey out of the oven and baste it one last time. Guests will be arriving shortly, and I'm making a huge effort to make sure everything is prepared and on the table by then. This is the first holiday I've spent with anyone since Grandma Rose died. Usually, I spent it eating a TV dinner while watching the Macy's Thanksgiving Parade. Jasen enters the kitchen with a look of exhaustion.

"I'm not sure if I can keep my eyes open," he says as he plops down on the barstool.

"That bad, huh?" I ask.

"Yup, it's getting harder and harder to get them to nap. One always cries and wakes up the other."

I giggle. "Thanks for getting them to sleep while I wrap up dinner."

Austin and Alexis have developed unique personalities already. Austin is quiet. He likes to reach for you, and he smiles a lot. Alexis is the completely opposite. She's a firecracker. Always crying. Always fussy. And barely smiles at all. Austin was born four minutes before Alexis, and I'm glad he decided to enter the world first. It makes me happy that Alexis will have a big brother to look after her, although something tells me she'll have him wrapped around her finger. I took them to Philly after they were born. I wanted them to meet their aunt.

"Everything smells good," Jasen says as his eyes scan the selection of food items I've prepared.

"Thank you, honey, and as soon as I add the icing on the cake, Thanksgiving dinner will be ready."

His grin is wide. "This is our first Thanksgiving dinner together."

"It is, and I'm excited to have your mom and Anthony over."

We sat Charlotte down and explained our story to her and Anthony. I thought she would be upset. After all, we did lie to her son. But she was understanding. She also said she had a feeling something was up with me that day we visited but couldn't put her finger on it. She comes over frequently, and we have a close relationship. I look at the time. "I'm going to go change. I'll be right back down."

I head upstairs to change into something more appropriate than the T-shirt and joggers I'm wearing. I enter my closet and scan the selection. I had Monroe's clothes put into storage. I just couldn't throw her things away. But there are a few pieces of hers that I kept. Like the plum sweater dress hanging to my right. I grab the dress and place it down on the bed. I decide to wear a pair of black ballet flats with it. I've been on my feet all day and refuse to suffer in a pair of heels. I decide to wear some jewelry. I don't own much of my own, so I decide to see what's in Monroe's jewelry chest. It's a holiday, and I want to look nice for our guests. I open the chest, and the first thing I see is an envelope with my name written on the front. I open it, and there's a letter inside. Tears fall as soon as I see her handwriting.

Morgan,

I decided to write you a letter while I wait for Cooper to arrive. If you're reading this now, it means I'm already gone. I've gone to travel the world. I had more cash stashed than I originally thought, so I should be able to get far. It's a good thing I've been stashing Jasen's money for years. Don't judge me. We're married, and what's his is mine, right? Anyway, I want to say that I'm sorry. I should have never asked you to switch with me. I should have owned up to my issues and done the right thing. But it's too late to turn back now. I know people will be hurt if this ever gets out. So, let's not let that happen, okay? I've never said this before, but I wish I could be more like you. You have a

heart of gold, sis. You're loyal. And you always consider
other people's feelings. But I'm just not that kind of
woman. I guess that's why you're my twin. To bring
balance to us. I know you have feelings for Jasen. And I
don't blame you. You're a better woman for him than what
I am. He probably should have belonged to you to begin
with. Maybe you would have made him happier. I never
loved him the way that he deserved. But you, I see how
much you care about him. How you want to protect his
heart and put your own selfishness aside. YOU are the kind
of woman he should be with, not me. If he ever finds out
what we've done, please tell him I'm sorry. Please tell him
that I did love him in my own weird way. I'm sorry I
couldn't be the woman he needed, but it's better this way.
I'm not angry about you two being together. After all, it
was my idea. MY WISH is for you two to be happy. Have
the life you both always wanted. I haven't decided what
state I'll end up in yet, but I'll call you as soon as I get there,
sis. I'll send you an address in case you want to visit, and
for the divorce papers I'm sure Jasen is going to file if he
ever learns what we did. I'm excited for this chapter in my
life, Morgan. I'll get to roam the earth, being free and doing
my own thing. It's what I've always wanted. Please tell
Cooper I'm sorry, but don't tell him where I am. And
Simone too if she ever learns the truth. I never meant to
hurt anyone, and if I could it all over again, I would.
Forgive me for all the times I hurt you. I might not have
had the courage to work on my failing marriage, but I
promise to be a better sister to you. I hope you know how
much I love you, Morgan. You're one half of me.

See you soon when I choose a state to settle in, Monroe
   Xoxo

By the time I'm done reading, the tears are falling at rapid speed. Jasen enters the room. "Hey, Mom just got here."

He crosses the room. "What's wrong?"

I open my mouth to tell him about the letter Monroe left behind, but the words don't come out. Instead, I sob. "Morgan, please, what is it?"

I shove the letter in his hands. He opens it up and starts to read it. His eyes glisten as he reads further. And when he's done, he looks up at me. "This was her goodbye. To both of us."

I nod. "She left it in her jewelry chest. It's been there all this time."

He pulls me into an embrace. "She knew you would make me happy, Morgan."

We hold each other tightly, each dealing with Monroe's words in our own way. My sister was able to tell me goodbye in a way. She was able to express remorse for her part in hurting those close to us. "We should put this away, for when the kids get older. They may want to read it after we tell them about her."

I nod. "I agree."

I start to walk away, but he grabs me. "Morgan, just for the record, I don't regret anything. I'm grateful for you. I'm grateful for our kids. This is the life I've always wanted."

I smile. "It's the life I've always wanted too. I guess Monroe got her wish, after all."

He looks up at the ceiling. "Yeah, I guess she did."

THE END

ABOUT THE AUTHOR

L.R. Jackson was born and raised on Maryland's eastern shore. She's a fun and spontaneous Gemini who has an addiction for wings and a passion for food. By day, she works in Corporate America, and by night, she dreams of Alpha Males and Romance, with her usual touch of suspense.

Writing has been a passion of hers since she was a little girl. She always knew that one day, she would share her stories with the world. Life got in the way, and her dream of writing was put on hold while she graduated from college and became a mom. But now, over twenty-five years later, she can proudly say that she's fulfilled her dream of becoming a published author.

When she's not playing chauffeur to her teenaged daughter, she can be found reading, cooking, traveling, and of course writing.

She has a huge appreciation for her readers and loves to hear from them. You may contact her via:

Facebook: Lewanda Jackson
Instagram: @mdgirl1979
Email: lewandaj@gmail.com
www.authorlrjackson.com

ALSO BY L.R. JACKSON

Royal Secrets

Haven

Institutionalized

The Call Girl

The Land of The Free??

www.ingramcontent.com/pod-product-compliance
Lightning Source LLC
Chambersburg PA
CBHW070319120726
47909CB00008B/2517